SECRET OF THE SERPENT

By
DON WILCOX

I0541432

ARMCHAIR FICTION
PO Box 4369, Medford, Oregon   97501-0168

*The original text of this novel was first
published by Ziff-Davis Publishing*

*For more information about Armchair Books and products, visit our
website at…*

www.armchairfiction.com

Or email us at…

armchairfiction@yahoo.com

WELCOME TO SPACE ISLAND

It was a strange planet adrift in space beyond the edge of the solar system. Its vegetation was lush, its atmosphere was pure, and it was home to the most bizarre life forms imaginable…

Bob Garrison awoke fitfully to find himself nearly submerged in a grimy stream in a deep, dark crevasse. He had forgotten everything about his former life. He had forgotten almost everything about his former planet…Earth. But in his new life as a serpent on this strange faraway world, he had already learned a great deal—including how to eat a human being in one bite!

FOR A COMPLETE SECOND NOVEL, TURN TO PAGE 117

CAST OF CHARACTERS

BOB GARRISON
He was a space pilot on a mission to a distant planet. He had no idea his life as a member of the human race was almost over.

FLORA HESSEL
This beautiful woman hated her ruthless, unprincipled boss, yet she played a pivotal role in his daring interplanetary scheme.

EMERSON HUNT
He was one of Earth's most respected scientists. Why had he isolated himself on a lonely planet in the depths of space?

ERNEST MACKLIN
All he wanted to do was take over a lucrative interplanetary business. So what if a few human lives got in the way.

KIPPER
He was no bigger than a pygmy, yet he was strong in mind and body—and he had carried a dark secret with him for 150 years!

THE WHITE HEAD
Who was this monstrous creature? And what strange power did it seem to hold over the entire populace of a planet?

DR. WINSTON
He was everything a young, brilliant doctor was supposed to be. Yet there was another force that seemed to control his destiny.

CHAPTER ONE

I STRAINED to keep my head out of the water as I floundered around in the blackness, trying to find a way out. The warm air smelled of blossoms and I think I should have been lulled back to sleep if it hadn't been for the water that kept rising around me. Sleep—how long had I been sleeping? How long had this complete blackness engulfed me? How did I happen to be here? Where did I come from? *Who was I? What was my name?*

A sickening feeling ran through the length of my long, coiled body. I didn't even know my own name. I had forgotten everything—everything that I was supposed to know in order to carry out my desperate purpose. *What* purpose?

WHAT PURPOSE?

I screamed within my mind like a woman falling to her death. There had been a purpose. An urgent purpose—something far more important than the life or death of any one man.

But how could I have a purpose relating to the life or death of any man when I was only a coiling, writhing mass of flesh, lost in some underground blackness, with an awful sleepiness engulfing me, and black water rising around me, and blossom-scented air lulling me into sickening illusions of nothingness.

I tried to fight the water back with my arms—*I had no arms—I had no legs*—and my efforts resulted in the random thrashing of my long, snakelike body.

I was a serpent!

I had been a man, and I had fallen through the dense purple clouds as a man—I was beginning to remember now. I had come to the ghastly Space Island, where the outcasts of the many planets were sent—to live or to die—and at the very minute that I had been sure I would land safely, I had suddenly fallen.

To die? No, to sink into a mire of blindness, deep in a crevasse, where no light from the heavens could penetrate. And there, in the slimy waters of a greenish-black stream, I had fought to keep my grip on those last few precious minutes of life. Bruised and battered, life's blood ebbing away, pain, pain, such burning pain, such child-like terror of the unknown that is death—and then—*merciful sleep*...

But now my consciousness was returning, sharp and sensitive, and my new snake-like body was finding ways to swim.

I swam cautiously, holding my serpent head just above the surface of the water. Presently a light broke through the deadly blackness—a streak of green, which skipped along the surface of the inky waters.

The ripples of green expanded. The cavern walls gradually changed from coal-black to rock-brown, and I lifted my head to look up through hundreds of feet of vertical surfaces. The planet's outer surface would be up there somewhere, perhaps a mile above the waters of this deep-cut stream. I was a prisoner—yes, twice a prisoner. A prisoner of the deep crevasse and a prisoner of some ghastly trick of nature that had given me this serpent's body.

I LOOKED back, now, and studied the forty-foot length of the purple and green body that was now my dwelling place. It was frightening and revolting and sickening, and I hated the sight of myself, and immediately I wished—

Oh, what a wish! What an awful thing to wish for! At that moment I was hating myself intensely.

I wished that I could frighten someone else! I wished to see someone else revolted and sickened by the flash of my green and purple tail through those black waters.

I would find someone!

It was a hideous purpose, but I was a serpent, and it was my purpose. I was no longer an honored emissary from the Earth who had come to the far-off Space Island with the purpose of *finding*—

WHAT WAS MY PURPOSE?

For a moment it had almost flashed back to me; but now it was gone again, and only the snake in which I dwelt could dominate my actions. I wanted to frighten someone, and so I swam through the twisting, sharp-edged passage.

Here the walls were only a few feet apart, and as I tried my luck at climbing I discovered the strength of my coils. In the dim light I saw, for the first time, the hundreds of folds that gave form and design to my yellowish-green belly. The wall's sharp edges prodded me with only trifling jabs of discomfort. It wasn't bad, this business of crawling. It came easy. I was beginning to like it.

"If you're a snake," I said to myself, *"you don't actually mind being a snake—"*

I was speaking half aloud, and my breathy hiss fascinated me. I tried it again.

"If you're a snake—snake—s-s-ssnake—*s-s-s-s-sss!*"

My hiss echoed up through the walls and there came an answer!

"Look out, down there!"

It was a human voice and it rang down through the walls like a fire alarm.

"Look out!" it cried. *"There's a monster!"*

Up through the hundreds of feet of jagged brown walls I caught sight of seven or eight tiny figures of human beings who were working at the upper end of a long rope. Then I saw, as my eyes followed downward to the near end of the line, the object of their warning cries. Two little men, clad in loincloths, had been lowered to a shelf of rock not fifty feet

7

away from where I was.

I say two *little* men, for they looked to me to be not more than two or three feet tall.

"Pygmies!" I said aloud. Then, with another satisfying hiss, "Pygmiessssss!"

The two little fellows were wild with fear at the sight of me. They clambered along the perilous ledge, trying to get back to the rope from which they had been lowered. I could see that they had been working with ropes and nets of their own, evidently trying to fish something out of the river.

Things happened fast, then, for my serpent instincts worked more powerfully than my human intelligence.

One of the pygmies slipped and fell. He struck the surface of the water with a splash. I could see him there in the deep green shadows, a black form bobbing up at the edge of the rock wall.

I slithered down to him; He screamed and struggled, but I caught him in the coils of my body and crushed him. Then my jaws opened wide and I took him in.

One quick, painful swallow and I got him down.

The men above were firing at me now, so I swam hard back into the darkness where their rays couldn't touch me. My belly was full, and I was comfortable and secure in my warm black waters. *Except* for the dull torture of my human conscience, I was *happy* to be a serpent.

CHAPTER TWO

THE first animal I met, other than the little human animals I had encountered in the river walls, was another monster, who like myself, was not quite at home in its hideous form. The very sight of it gave me a great deal of mental trouble.

If I had had no more mind than an ordinary serpent I

might not have suffered any agony whatever. I might have attacked it, and either it would have killed *me,* or I would have killed *it.*

But that bothersome streak of human intelligence that I still possessed—the remnant of my previous existence, which was still haunting me—helped me realize something very important about this new monster.

It helped me realize that it, too, was a person who had been transformed.

I first saw it on the rim of the crevasse during the morning that I found my way to the top. I had climbed through the long, long night, by the light of six different moons—or neighboring planets, I couldn't be sure which. These heavenly bodies had crossed over the deep gash that had imprisoned me for so many hours, and each time I caught sight of one, sailing slowly across my thin line of sky, I felt compelled to climb, faster and faster.

Each time one of them passed on, out of sight, I felt weak and exhausted from my effort and wished that I were again at the surface of the water. I belonged in the water. I was safe there. No, there was another moon sliding into sight—I must climb up toward it faster, faster!

When light at last began to gray the sky with morning, I was sure that the night had lasted for scores and scores of Earth hours, and I knew that there would also be a very long day ahead. It wouldn't be wise for me to start back through the deep descent until I had at least found some nourishment. Somewhere there must be more pygmies. I kept my eyes sharpened for the sight of any movement along the surface of the rocky ledge. And there, in the pink light of dawn *I saw it.*

It was large, for a cat—large enough to be a draft horse or a small elephant—but that wasn't what made it such a weird and formidable sight to my eyes. It had two heads, and its four eyes, always turned in the same direction were casting their baleful greenish-yellow glare glow at me as I ascended.

The cat-like body hardly moved. I might have expected it to bound away in fear, but it stood its ground. My coils carried me up through the last twenty feet of ascent and I worked my way, as limber as any earthworm, along the edge.

The double-headed cat-monster watched me with its four steady eyes. When my flipping tail struck a loose stone and sent it clattering down through the crevasse, the cat-monster didn't wink an eye, but simply went on staring at me. The hair began to rise on its back. Its claws emerged, thin white lines that spoke a warning.

I stopped, holding my head about four feet above the surface of the boulder upon which my chest—if it could be called a chest—had crawled to a stop. I drew my head back a few inches and slowly opened my jaws.

The cat-monster's shoulders hunched dangerously, and the beast showed his saber teeth.

JUST then the slight rustle of feet sounded from a heap of rocks to my left, and I turned in time to see the first shot fired. The tongues of red flame darted out from the muzzles of three guns.

Pygmies again!

They were shooting at the cat-monster! One blast—two—three! Deadly rays of *zeego* fire. I had seen enough of it on the Earth, I should know. Whoever the pygmies were, they possessed *zeego* ray guns that had certainly come from Earth.

My human impulse was to leap over the rocks and pounce upon the little men with my fists swinging. But human impulses were only a handicap to my new body. It worked on principles of its own, and instantly I was crawling at high speed.

With fangs bared, I pounced upon the surprised trio.

Three *zeego* guns dropped. Two of the pygmies were running down a cliff path as hard as they could go. Their feet thudded with a fancy little rhythm that reminded me of a military drum I had heard somewhere. The other sound was the scream of the third pygmy, whose voice might have been compared to a screech of a clarinet in high register. It ended with a gurgling, choking sound as my coiling body closed around him.

One's serpent habits take hold quickly, I found. Without debating the matter, I simply gulped him down.

I would have given the other two a hard chase, then, if it hadn't been for another cry that chilled my cold blood. The monster-cat—in pain—dying? I wondered. It had certainly been struck by the rays of *zeego* fire. I slithered back over the rocks to the cliff's edge.

The creature had been struck across both of its foreheads, just above the four eyes—four greenish-yellow eyes that were wide with pain and terror.

The lids all began to close simultaneously; for a moment I thought the cat-monster was dying. Its shoulders sank and it went down, and it was shrinking—

Shrinking, smaller and smaller—crying with pain—crying with the voice of a girl—

It was transforming into something—something more nearly human. Its two heads were growing smaller. Its body was losing the fur covering, growing whiter. Pink shoulders came into sight. Human arms were forming, clasping the breasts of its human body and then it was running from me, from one projecting rock to another, until it had hidden somewhere in the crags.

I watched, not daring to follow.

When it looked out, peering cautiously through the clump of bushes at the foot of the crags, I saw that its arms and shoulders were those of a beautiful girl. Its two heads had been reduced in size to correspond with its human body, but they were not human heads. They were feline heads, in every detail, and their four cat-like eyes were all watching me with deadly suspicion.

I went back to where the three *zeego* ray guns had fallen and wondered how I could manage to pick them up and use them.

CHAPTER THREE

IT WAS a strange world I was in, a world in which no new arrival could know his rights. In the first place he couldn't be sure that he knew *himself.* In the second place, he couldn't be sure of his own eyes when he *tried* to know his neighbors. In the third place, *how* could he be sure that anything he *did* know for sure today would be the *same* tomorrow?

I must admit—perhaps sarcastically—that this serpent was tying himself in knots, almost literally, for many hours to come.

Finding a pool of water, I would look in and see my new face reflected there and for a moment I would despise myself. Those evil yellowish eyes that I saw in the reflection were enough to make anyone hate and distrust me. The fine scales around my nose and jaws were almost as sly as my eyes, the way they would catch the tints from the rocks and trees and flowers. I knew that I *could* lurk in a pool where the pygmies came to pick the brilliant orange-colored water flowers—the *flopetals*—and I *could* catch enough protective coloration that a pygmy wouldn't see me until I sprang. I was sure I *could*, and if I ever got hungry enough I *would*.

But my powers as a serpent, as I have already hinted, were the source of much mental torture. It was bad enough to possess an animal instinct that would cause me to kill and devour little human beings. It was even worse to realize that these people must somehow be connected to my former self, as proved by the fact that (a) they were human and (b) they talked English and (c) they used Earthmen's weapons.

Probably you've never had an occasion to eat a human being. But if you have, you know that *after* your stomach is filled and your soul is again at peace with the world, *then* you can feel all sorts of remorse for your evil deed.

I was remorseful regularly about every twelve hours. But just as regularly, too, I became quite hungry—and at such times I was guilty of hoping, with all of my forty-foot being, that the supply of pygmies wouldn't run out.

I hoped, too, that they wouldn't get too handy with their *zeego* guns. As a serpent, I had certain responsibilities that needed to be carried out faithfully. One of them was to take care of my prisoner.

I'm speaking of *her*.

Yes, *she* was my prisoner, and I was taking care of her. I was protecting her, too. Whenever I thought the pygmies were in danger of discovering her hiding place, I found a way to warn her that they were coming.

It seemed her two cat-like heads were always alert to my coming. Whenever I came crawling along the cliff path toward the cavern pool where she lived, I would hear her plunge into the water, and that was proof that she had heard me coming. Then I would see her—those two heads of hers—swimming along quietly to the narrow opening in the wall of rock. Somehow it reminded me of a corner in a well-planned zoo, for it was a perfect retreat from the passing public. The public, in this case, being a forty-foot purple and green serpent.

So it was, that I kept her a prisoner, and cared for her, and came to think of her more as a pair of untamed cats, joined by a whimsy of nature into a single body. Either the water or the cave would conceal her body from my eyes, as a rule, and

I ceased to think of her as having human qualities.

At first I had tried a few times to talk with her; but neither of her heads had offered any answers. I lapsed into a more frequent use of my warning hisses, consequently, and began to neglect my serpent's efforts to talk English.

ONE day—which is to say, many, many hours after this very strange life had begun—something happened that changed everything almost with the speed of light.

A crippled spaceship came hurtling down out of the sky, and when it fell within five hundred feet of the surface it exploded outward into dozens of pieces, like a shell bursting. The pieces must have scattered over at least a five-mile radius, and there wasn't much chance, I assumed, that any band of half civilized pygmies would ever pick them up. And I was right.

But I was wrong in thinking that this rain of wreckage would go unnoticed.

From a mountain peak about thirty miles away a whole squadron of planes came out to circle back and forth across the valley, and I knew that there was someone in these parts who was more concerned with this hail of trouble than the pygmies. Fifteen planes hummed over, as slowly as a hawk soars over a field in search of a mouse.

They came in low over the edge of the crevasse.

I crawled back into a clump of bushes where I wouldn't be seen. I could see the two cat heads at the mouth of the small cave, so I knew that *she* was watching too.

"Don't let them see you," I called. It was the first time I had spoken in English in some time. *She* looked at me and folded her white arms tighter. She moved deeper into the water so that only two pink noses and four yellow eyes remained above the surface.

A few minutes later the plane drifted directly over the

small pool. By this time I had guessed that they were looking down upon every bit of lake or rivulet or feeder stream that cascaded into the deep crevasse. Why, I would learn later.

One of the planes circled back over the little pool. By this time *she* was back in the cave, and I felt reasonably sure that they hadn't seen either one of us. But they threw out a package as they went over and it fell toward the pool.

It burst just before it struck. It burst like a cloud of flour—or better, sulfur, for it was creamy yellow in color. It struck the surface of the water, and there was a bubbling, arid hissing of steam.

Then I heard *her* cry.

I tried to interpret the wail as that of two voices, not one. There was no reason, I thought, that one of the voices should cry and not the other. Yet I somehow knew, in spite of the spine-chilling echoes of the cavern, that it was only one voice. And not a feline voice, either. It was the cry of a girl.

Instantly I plunged into the pool. It was the first time that I had tried to approach *her* since that first morning when I had seen her as a dangerous furry monster. The whirl of steam blinded me for a moment, and the fumes caught in my lungs and seemed to burst out through my chest—if I could call it a chest—and thudded out like pounding hammers at my shoulders—

My *shoulders?*

The fumes stung my lungs, and the steam burned at my eyes, and then suddenly it was over and the air was clear, and there was the pool of blue water, with my long snake-like body showing green and purple through the waves.

I was ashamed to be there, so close, then. For the *girl* in the cave before me thought I was being ill mannered to intrude upon *her.*

The *girl?* Yes, with the same white arms folded tightly over her breasts. The light from the sky kissed her pink shoulders. She moved down a little deeper into the water, so that only her head—her beautiful human head, with flowing dark hair, a pair of frightened dark eyes, and lips parted in speechless wonderment—showed above the surface of the water.

I *knew* this person. I had seen her before. Where? When? If I could only remember how this had all come about—

She spoke, then, breathlessly.

"Look, Bob, you have *arms* now," she said. Then, "You *are* Bob, aren't you?"

CHAPTER FOUR

BEFORE I had a chance to answer, she cried, "Hide quick! They're coming!"

The hum of planes was on us almost without warning. I made a dart toward the cave—*her* cave—and at the same instant I caught sight of my own reflection in the water—my vicious-looking eyes! That was what turned me back. As a serpent I didn't trust myself to invade her private refuge. I whirled about, and the water splashed high around the rocky walls.

"Quick! Get out of sight!" she cried.

I crawled faster than I had ever crawled before. I headed toward a clump of bushes. I knew I could reach them before the planes spotted me. But I was moving far too quickly. With my serpent's head whirling to keep watch on their approach, I missed my direction and plunged back into the crevasse!

My human arms grabbed frantically at the ragged edge of rock. What a futile gesture! My muscular forty-foot body was racing too fast to be caught by a thin pair of arms. I rolled into the opening.

As I fell, I caught myself momentarily on the first ledge.

My head and neck fought to catch around the rocky projections, and my hands grasped frantically at the walls for a hold. But the bulk of my body was already falling, like the loops of a cable, and if I had tried to hold fast I would surely have snapped my head off.

It was a strange thought for my mind to feed upon as I fell. Some boyhood experience was coming back to me. In the fields—in the pastures—somewhere long ago on a more friendly planet...the Earth. The snakes of those fields may have been friendly, but I was a boy and a snake was a snake, and I had used to kill them by grabbing their tails and cracking them like a whip to break their necks.

I was falling, falling, down and down through nearly a mile of rocky walls. I was turning, writhing, twisting, trying to widen my coiled body to catch like a steel spring within the narrowing walls.

Rip!

The curve of my side struck a projection, and the green and purple pattern tore with a gash of red.

Within a hundred feet of the bottom, I managed to straighten out my body so that the loop was in a vertical plane, and the wall burns were avoided.

Splasssssssh!

What an echo went up and down the crevasse. I sank under instantly but still I heard its sound, and it seemed that the greenish-black waters were alive with the sounds for minutes afterward.

When my head emerged and I again began to breathe the soft blossom-filled air, my first thought was of the girl. She had called me *Bob*.

Was I Bob?

What had made her think that I was anything more than a slimy reptile?

The thought was too much for me, burdened as I was by a

water-spanked belly and a torn side. I relaxed and failed to find the stamina I needed to keep my consciousness from ebbing away. I fainted away into serpent's sleep.

CHAPTER FIVE

WHEN I awakened, the moons were sliding slowly over my tiny streak of sky. There would be hours of night before I should be able to see any human figures at the top of the opening. And I was hungry.

"I'm *hungry*," I said aloud. "It's good that *she* isn't here now."

When you speak aloud, that way, you always stop and wonder whether someone might have heard you. Maybe that's what gave me the weird feeling that someone had heard, and that I was in the presence of company. I tried not to rustle the waves as I stretched my neck and peered into the surrounding darkness. I listened. Nothing but the low gurgle of water and an occasional complaining murmur of my empty intestinal tract.

I made a disheartening discovery, then, and I groaned aloud. I wondered how a mountain climber would feel if he got almost to the top and then skidded on the ice and slid all the way back and had to start over.

It had taken me hours and hours of work to get to the top the first time, and here I was back in the depths again. But that wasn't all. *My arms and hands were gone!*

With a commendable human impulse to forego the pleasure of feasting on a pygmy (since none were likely to be handy before daybreak) I had decided to try this stream for clams or fish. There must be something, I thought, or the pygmies wouldn't have been down here with nets. But my inspiration was blasted by my discovery. My shoulders had shrunken into slight lumps where my cylindrical body enlarged below my neck. All traces of the appendages had disappeared.

Hunting clams or fish without the aid of hands wasn't going to be easy. My serpent's instinct urged me not to plow through the water with my mouth open.

I tried to think of a way out, but I was too hungry to think. I needed a pygmy. I was too weak and sore to start the journey back to the surface, nearly a mile overhead. I wondered…didn't any pygmies ever get lost on their way home from a celebration and tumble into this place by mistake? I didn't wish them any ill luck, and still—

The thought heartened me and I began to swim, slowly, painfully, up the stream. It soon occurred to me that I might be spending much of my immediate future at the bottom of this weird crevasse, so I decided it would do well to explore as much of the stream as possible.

Curious, the sensations that accompanied me through that long night. A few minutes of moonlight filtered all the way down to my bright eyes and gave them a frightening yellow glow in the water's reflection. After the moonlight came darkness. Cloudy darkness, and rain. Thin drops that splashed over the length of my coils as I raised one loop after another of my rope-like body to the surface. The sky again, then the moon again. And once more…that mystifying feeling that someone else was present.

"Maybe it's the ghost of one of those pygmies I ate," I said aloud. I listened, unmoving, trying to determine whether my words had been answered with an ever so delicate sound—the amused puff of breath from some listener back in the darkness.

I swam faster. Suddenly I stopped and allowed the waters to swirl around me. I listened. I *did* hear the sounds of breathing. No—it was *whispering!*

IT SEEMED as if the sound was almost over the top of me. Then it retreated. I waited several moments, listening closely, but it was gone.

I was tempted to follow, but which direction? A human whisper was a promise of food for a hungry serpent. But I was puzzled as to how any follower could somehow be hovering over me.

As I contemplated the possibilities, I slowly formed a plan. It was a plan that would depend on finding a sharp turn in the river and making sure that I didn't give myself away.

I plowed ahead, increasing my speed rapidly. The narrow line of night sky, high above me, was darkening again. In a few seconds I came to a sharp turn that I knew would hide me—at least momentarily—from any possible pursuer. Swishing through the turn, I applied my muscled coils to the wall and climbed up.

I slipped out of the water almost silently so there was no warning splash. I bridged between the walls less than twenty feet above the stream's surface. The humps that would have been my shoulders rested against one side, and the coil of my belly braced solid against the other. Thus, my head and neck were free to move back and forth between the walls.

In a moment it came—a length of rope with a weight on the lower end. *I knew it!* My pursuer—or rather, *pursuers*—hung from a rope that was being moved by some guiding force *nearly a mile up*, at the top of the crevasse.

The rope rubbed against my unseen body. The occupants of the swing at the lower end coasted to a stop and dangled like an uncertain pendulum.

"What's happening?" one of them whispered.

"We're caught on something," said the other voice. "We'd better get loose or he'll get away. He was swimming fast."

"Are you sure it was *him?* It might be the girl, you know."

"If it was a serpent, it's more likely to be a man. Here,

let's kick the wall together and maybe we'll jar loose." There was a momentary pause, followed by some scraping noises against the wall. Then the voice spoke again. "Wait a minute...I can see something right above us. Looks like it bridges all the way across. Where's the light?"

"We don't dare show a light," said the other voice urgently. "That beast wouldn't know whether we were a friend or foe, and what's more, he wouldn't care."

That was when I broke my long silence with an ugly hissing question.

"Whicccch are you?"

I felt the jerk of the rope as it scraped past an injured spot on my body and instantly pulled away from me. The two men must have held close contact with their guides high overhead. Whatever their signal system, they swung back from me quickly before I could dart forward with my head. They swung back and up, without stopping for a word of response.

"What's the hurry?" I hissed.

One of them called back, "Who are you?"

I didn't know. The girl had called me Bob, and the name had begun to ring pleasantly. I had caught the impression that it was all right to be Bob, as far as she was concerned, but that it might not be so good to be anyone else. I wondered.

"Bring me some food," I called.

"Who *are* you?" the voice returned.

"How do *I* know?" I said. "I'm too hungry to know anything."

There was a short whispered consultation. Should they flash the light on or shouldn't they? Would the monster snap at them or would he give them a chance? The wisps of conversation were reassuring, and I began to know that these two meant to be friends, if I would give them a chance.

"Are you *Bob?*" one of them asked presently.

"Who is *Bob?*" I asked.

THEY put their heads together again. If I didn't know who Bob was, maybe I wasn't one of the party they were seeking after all. Maybe I hadn't come to Space Island recently—maybe I was an old-timer here who had simply kept myself well hidden until yesterday when I had been lured to the surface by the sight of the two-headed cat-woman. It was all a mystery to me, but I wasn't going to turn away any advantage or miss a chance to eat.

"Pull me up to the surface," I said, "so I can find my dinner." I put considerable hiss in my voice as I added, "Otherwise I'll have to eat what I find down here."

"Meaning what?" one of the voices asked sharply.

"Meaning you. *Hssssssh. You.*"

The rustle from the swing above was the sound of two men making ready for trouble with ray pistols.

"All right, fellow," one of them said. "Crawl up this way and twine yourself around the rope. We'll take you up to the surface. No false moves, though, or you'll never eat another dinner."

I obeyed. My long body swished quietly upward between the walls and I crossed over to the rope. A moon slipped into sight, high above, and the two men below me must have had a fair view of me as I corkscrewed upward. My sore belly was put to a cruel test, trying to hold a grip on a rope no bigger around than a man's arm, but presently I was fully entwined and I gave them the signal to take me up...easy.

And up we went.

A few minutes later I slithered over the edge of the crevasse once more, and mentally I vowed I would never seek those lower regions again. A feeling of relief washed over me as I momentarily laid motionless on the upper surface.

I was beginning to feel a sense of purpose again. But what could it possibly be? All the way up through the dark walls I had tried my best to recall what it was. Someone I must find? That seemed somewhere close to the truth, I thought.

Someone to find—the only someone I knew up here was the beautiful girl in the pool. Well, there was the one purpose that I could swear to. I wanted to know whether she was still there, and who she was, and where I had known her before.

"Bob," she had called me. If words ever echoed in a snake's ears, it was hers. If any serpent ever felt obliged to go back to a beautiful woman and find out why she had dared to trust him as far as she had trusted me, I was that serpent.

And so, out of these purposes, half defined, and half foggy, I acted with the slyness of a snake.

I could see the outline of a small plane on the ground. In the light of the various moons, I could see that its door was open. Did I dare?

The rope was still rising. I looked up. It was being wound into a blimp that hovered darkly over the crevasse. The men had just reached the edge of the crevasse. They stepped toward me. I knew they would expect to take me in charge, using their pistols to command me.

"This way, you. If you want that dinner—"

I didn't listen. Something from my half-forgotten memories told me that I knew how to handle a plane, and the door was open. It was a perfect set-up if I could crawl in before the guns started heading me off with red fire.

Swissssh. Zipppp! I shot along over the cool grass and I ploughed right into the plane's entrance.

There—so far so good. I pushed my nose against a lever that locked me in. The men were rushing toward the plane, shouting. The lines of red fire were *zeego* shots, the same as the pygmies had used. But they were outside and I was safe within, crawling across the floor to the controls.

Could I, with my serpent's nose, my teeth, my hammer-like head, my agile neck—could I get away with it?   In another moment I would know.

If it worked, then I would have the freedom to see what this strange land was all about.   And first of all I would find that girl, if they hadn't taken her already.   A moment later a feeling of despair rushed through me.

The controls were locked!

Not a thing responded to my touch.   Not a switch—

But suddenly, as I was trying one gadget after another with my tongue, the overhead lights came on—surely not from anything I had done...

"There," came a voice through the speaker, "I guess we're ready to take him with us."   Those were voices from the blimp coming in on the intercom.

"Is he in?" another voice asked.

"He crawled right in without any coaxing," said one of the voices that had come up from the depths with me.   "That would seem to prove that he is indeed Bob.   Look...he's even fumbling at the controls.   It's a good bet he's our missing pilot all right; and if he is, then it's another victory for us, boys.   We're getting the party assembled gradually."

So I was Bob, a pilot.   All right, if they said so, I'd be agreeable.   But I was also a hungry serpent.   I wasn't a cooperative animal.   I was sly and vicious, and all I wanted was to look out for myself.   If they thought they were going to fly me somewhere as a prisoner, they had another thing coming.   I coiled around and crawled back to the door and nosed against the lever.

It wouldn't open.

Then the plane started moving—moving steadily through the blackness.   Then it began to rise—slowly at first, and then more quickly.   I could hear the howl of the wind rushing over the plane's outer surface.   They were flying it by remote control, and I was on my way to *somewhere*, whether I liked it or not.

CHAPTER SIX

NO DOUBT about it, they had set a neat trap for me. And here I had thought that I was being the sly one. They may have had the advantage of human looks, but they had certainly out-serpented the serpent.

We went toward the pink dawn and landed in the early morning twilight on a shelf of concrete in the upper level of a valley between two huge shoulders of mountain. Here was the stronghold from which I had seen the planes come not so many hours ago, after the explosion of the falling spaceship.

My plane landed and came to a stop in front of a magnificent arched entrance. The other planes and the blimp closed in around me, and a ground crew of blue and orange men came out to take over.

The door of my plane was not opened until a glass and metal cage was set up for me.

I crawled in without any undue coaxing. Their trickery was still working. They had put a pygmy in the far corner of the cage. I *thought* it was a pygmy. But when my jaws clamped over it I found that it was a wax imitation. I spat it out and recoiled to strike back at someone. I didn't care whom. However, the door of my cage had already slid shut and I was caught.

If I had been an honored ambassador from the Earth, extending good will and a promise of interplanetary trade to this planet, I'm sure my hosts would have found it in their power to feed me without any undue delay. And I would have eaten, and a friendship would have been sealed then and there, by virtue of the universal law of brotherhood that springs from a full stomach.

But I was a serpent in a cage, and neither my human voice nor the growlings of my lank intestines could prod my caretakers to move any faster than they wished to do.

"Is he ready for the experiment?" I heard someone ask.

"Better take him back into the Z Lab," came the answer.

Not bad looking scientists, I thought to myself. Plump and well fed and sufficiently healthy to keep a hungry serpent nourished for a week. What other attributes these men may have had didn't interest me much at the time. I had caught a fleeting glimpse of the arched doorway, a noble structure ornamented with polished brass, large enough for planes to enter. Of the three openings under the arch, I was taken through the one that served the automotive traffic. Two trucks spun past me on their way out to one of the mountain highways, and I saw that they were driven *by pygmies!*

"This isn't going to be so pleasant," I told myself. "Now how many of these little fellows will I have to account for when they bring me up before the judge?"

I was counting back over my indiscretions, shall we say, when the tunneled driveway opened into a lighted room. They wheeled me past a row of elevators, on through a lobby of automotive vehicles, and at last through a door of three square green-metal panels marked *Laboratory Z.*

The room would have been perfectly dark if someone hadn't been meddling with a lightning machine. As soon as the lab door closed behind me, the lightning was vividly apparent. It would have captured anyone's attention. Dark-dark-dark-*flash!* Dark-dark-dark-*flash!*

After the first fifteen purplish-white flashes I began to catch the rhythm and could tell when the next flash was coming. But that was an illusion. *Flash-flash-flash!* All at once they were coming fast, and I had a premonition that they were going to close in and electrocute me. I couldn't tell exactly where the lightning was coming from. But all at once

I saw the door of my cage fly open. No one was standing there with guns—it was my chance.

I flashed around and darted out through the opening. My flying tail struck the rear wall as I turned, only to add a hard push to my sudden effort to slither out while there was a chance.

Would I ever learn?

It was nothing more than a trick, of course.

I REALIZED it the moment the last of my forty-foot body found the cool concrete floor. The very next flash showed a derrick-like arm swinging down from the ceiling. One glimpse—the resemblance was unmistakable—it was a package of sulfur-colored powders, the same as those that had descended on the girl in the pool.

Floooof!

At that instant the blackness of the room gave way to what seemed a luminous dust storm. My serpent-like form writhed and whipped and scraped—and fought. The deluge was over me. I coughed and choked with wild unspeakable tortures.

It was over. The air was clearing, and the steam that had stung deep in my lungs was melting away. Bars of lights came on around the room, and the first thing I saw was my own form in a huge mirror.

I moved, half crawling and half *walking,* toward the mirror.

If you can imagine the classical facade of an old fashioned colonial home, with two pairs of fifty-foot columns standing white and solid on either side of the entrance, that's the sort of frame I now approached. It was the highest mirror I had ever seen. A full-sized giraffe could have used it to advantage and still had room to spare.

I moved up the six wide concrete steps with considerable pride in my bearing. You see, I was watching myself in the mirror, fully aware that something had transformed me. *I had two arms once more, and also a good pair of human legs.*

The arms, somewhat to my dismay, were about six feet long—long enough that I had at once begun to use them for front legs. My snake-like body was still all there, from my scaled face and sly greenish-yellow eyes all the way down to my brightly colored tail. But I had legs! I was walking as well as crawling.

"How do you like it?"

The voice came out of a speaker in the wall.

"How did you do it?" I replied. I looked around to see who was conversing with me, and I spied them—three men in a plexiglass pillbox on the opposite wall.

"Come over this way so we can see I you," one of the men said. "Do you remember who you are?"

"Of course," I said. "I'm Bob Garrison, a registered spaceship pilot. I came to Space Island on an errand—"

I checked myself. After all, it was none of their concern, so far as I knew. Just now I was whirling with more thoughts than I could hold, but it wouldn't do to spill any of the confidential ones. I was not too sure, after all, that I was among friends.

"I'm Bob Garrison," I repeated.

"Walk around the room, Bob Garrison," came the order.

I didn't mind obeying. It paid to know what one's body would and would not do, and if this was going to be my body for awhile—well, I needed a bit of exercise to get my balance.

All at once the hunger pangs shot through me, and I stopped immediately below the platform where the three men were perched and looked up at them. Then the dreadful fact of my pygmy dinners came back with a new surge of remorseful conscience. It was awful. It was hideous. It was terrifying, and my serpent blood ran cold at the thought.

There I was, however, caught between the human impulse

to recover my civilized feelings and my bestial instincts to leap up at the platform and devour one of those men.

I LEAPED. I leaped and struck at the plexiglass enclosure, and almost hit it.

"Good action," one of the men mumbled through the speaker. "I can't recall that we've ever had such a specimen as this before."

"I don't understand," another scientist replied, "why he shouldn't have transformed more completely into his original stage. He seems to have regained the human memory, all right. And we're not going to have any trouble bringing his arms back to normal. But he's taken a pretty deep shock, somehow, to have that serpent's body fixed upon him so stubbornly. How large a dose of powders did we apply?"

Their discussion went on along these lines for several moments. The girl, they mentioned, had transformed back to normal with only half as strong an exposure as they had given me. But someone pointed out that she had already been partially reconverted by means of a shock from *zeego* gunfire.

"Why don't we try the *zeego* fire on this one, then?"

That matter consumed a few minutes' earnest discussion, and two or three times I was sure they would decide to do it. (Once, not so many hours ago, I had captured three *zeego* guns of my own, I recalled, and had tried to find a pygmy to use them on, but in the end my appetite had always won over my scientific ambitions.) They eventually suspended their discussion. The person in charge would need to be consulted before they did anything more to me.

"He's a pretty valuable specimen, just as he stands," said the chief spokesman. "We might ruin him with *zeego* fire. I have a hunch—"

He paused as if perhaps he should hold back his confidences, but the other two consultants were already guessing his thought.

"Yes, gentlemen, I have a hunch that Dr. Hunt will prefer to dissect this specimen as he now stands. An undamaged skeleton of this sort will give us one of the finest studies in the laboratory."

So that was it! I was to be an undamaged skeleton for Dr. Hunt was I? It was too much.

And then it came back to me: I was the man who had come to this ghastly outpost in outer space on a secret mission, if you please—*to rescue the lost scientist, Dr. Emerson Hunt.*

I leaped and struck the underside of the transparent enclosure so hard that the floor cracked, and a brace tore loose from its wall mooring. The three gentlemen must have decided to take their conference elsewhere. They made a quick exit and locked the wall door behind them.

CHAPTER SEVEN

I SHALL be everlastingly thankful to the caretaker who fed me before my visit with Flora Hessel. I was ravenous, and I simply couldn't have maintained any outward appearance of civilized serpenthood if they hadn't fed me.

The cage was around me again. I didn't mind that. It was just the protection I needed while I did some tall thinking. Flora Hessel, bless her heart, came to me and helped me think. With her help, it all seemed worthwhile.

"We were both warned against coming to this outpost in the first place," she said.

I nodded. I was thinking how beautiful a person she was, even dressed in one of the workmen's uniforms—a rough one-piece suit of blue and orange and a liberal sprinkling of grease spots. Her dark hair was loosely combed, falling free over one shoulder. Her bare legs and arms were lithe and graceful as she settled herself comfortably in the chair that a caretaker provided for her outside my cage.

"I remember what you said, Bob," she smiled, "when they warned you against coming. You said you had your own good reason for coming—something more than hiring on as their pilot, I was sure. But you never told me."

"No, I've never told anyone," I said cautiously. I had been on the verge of telling her more than once during our long hours of flight together. But Ernest Macklin had done his very best to keep us from becoming acquainted. Macklin had hired each of us for our specialized jobs, and he had intended that we should keep our minds on our work.

"We had heard tales of these strange transformations before we came," Flora went on, looking dreamily off into space. "Don't know about you, but until now I simply didn't believe they could happen."

"I didn't quite realize," I admitted.

"Still, that was the very earliest report that ever came out of this planet—you know—after the first wave of settlers from Earth were expelled from Mars…"

It could be found in any modern history book, even though each historian was careful to word his account in such a way that the story could be taken as a legend rather than fact. The first wave of American and English settlers on the Earth colonies of Mars had gone through the bitter ordeal of becoming adjusted to new climatic and gravitational conditions, and the awful experience had taken its toll. Fifty years after the first wave of settlers, the second wave had come to Mars in great numbers. They came equipped with better means of setting up conditions congenial to their own needs, and they made a healthy go of it.

But the second group of Martian settlers simply couldn't endure the first! That was the original tragedy—and this was the fact that every writer of history deplored. The first group had become so changed and twisted in their physical and emotional characteristics—shrunken in mind and body, and animal-like in their tastes—that in a sudden act of hysteria the second group had loaded up hundreds of the first group on derelict spaceships and simply rocketed them *out of the solar system!*

Beyond the solar system, they had fallen to this mysterious planet, Space Island, where the forces of gravitation had been found to be much like those of Earth. The drifting planet's inner heat provided conditions suitable for life, and there was life here—life in innumerable forms. Although no sun hung in the sky, there were regular periods of night and day caused by an atmospheric phenomenon that was still scientifically unexplained. Since much of the interplanetary driftwood, living and otherwise, from the solar system and three other systems, found its way to this particular catch-all in the sky, it was not surprising that there would be many forms of life here.

But, according to the fanciful legend that the historians handled with great caution, those varying forms of life were the results of *transformations* that occurred as soon as the creatures from other planets began to eat the food and drink the water that Space Island provided.

And according to the legend, the first outcasts from the Earth colony on Mars were still living here—not their descendants, but the original members of the first group. If this were true, they must be men and women more than two hundred years of age—or *were* they men and women?

Or were they *beasts* who roamed the mountains of Space Island?

THE historians could only cite the legend and promise that in time scientists would have more answers.

But many scientists were not eager to come, considering

the odds that a personal tragedy of some sort would strike them before they had time to set up their laboratories and initiate their research plans. Not many on Earth knew the truth of the situation, but the famed Dr. Hunt had come to Space Island not of his own accord. There had been a bit of smooth interplanetary gangsterism in back of his sudden departure from the well-known Emerson Laboratories.

All of this background came welling up into my thoughts while I talked with Flora Hessel from my metal and glass cage. The recent liberation from the awful serpent-thoughts gave me a flare of new hope, that I might still be on the trail of my original purpose.

"I am going to confide in you," I said quietly, trying my best to keep the hiss out of my voice. "But first, you must tell me something. How did you know, when you first saw me as a serpent, that I might be Bob? Why didn't you guess me to be Ernest Macklin? Or Pete Hogan? Or one of the others?"

"Don't you know?"

"There were over ten of us on board," I said, "and certainly some of the others must have been transformed into something unrecognizable. I certainly didn't recognize you when you were in your two-headed "cat body." It wasn't until you began to reduce into human form—and even then my mind was too bleary to remember exactly who you were. I only knew that I felt friendly toward you."

"That was it," said Flora. "It was your manner—your friendliness and your courage. You remember when you rushed after those little gunmen the minute they started shooting? Pete Hogan wouldn't have done that."

"But Ernest Macklin might have. After all, he's the one who employed you to come up here in the first place. He wouldn't want to see you shot down after investing in you."

She smiled at the corners of her eyes. "You're right. If

they'd killed me, he'd have shaken the gold out of my teeth to line his pocketbook."

"But you knew that I was Bob, not Ernest Macklin? Are you sure I'm *not* Macklin?"

"You were quite considerate of me while I was cornered in that cavern pool," she said. "For a snake, you used remarkably nice manners. Macklin wouldn't have been that decent even at his human best. You know that."

I must admit that her words were pleasing to me, and I felt that I was better acquainted with her than I had been at any time during the trip. Macklin had tried to drive a wedge between the two of us from the start. He had warned me that she was a dangerous person—that she had once very nearly become a gangster's moll—that she had been mixed up in a gang war that had resulted in five killings one dark night on the West Side of the Bronx. But I knew that whatever her past had been, she had later gained an enviable reputation from her social service work with the tough, homeless men from the same area of the city. It was said that she could walk into a mob of quarreling, angry men and have them singing hymns within a few minutes.

That was why Ernest Macklin had hired her for this job, as I had learned from their conversations on the ship. He was lining this planet up for some high-powered commercial venture, and he wanted the inhabitants—the *human* inhabitants—to be at least docile enough that they wouldn't obstruct the march of his progress.

JUDGING from what I had seen of those devilish pygmies, her task wasn't going to be easy. Moreover, if there were many freaks like me, half-animal and half-human, little Miss Hessel was going to have a big handful of trouble.

"Do they consider you a prisoner here?" I asked.

"I'm not sure," she looked wistfully at the window and the

ridge of green mountains beyond. "They seem to think they're going to find Ernest Macklin somewhere, though it beats me how they can find any trace of a lost person on such a big, wild planet."

"And if they find Macklin—?"

"Well, I've told them I'm contractually bound to work for him. I signed the contract and took out life insurance before I boarded."

"I wonder what *he* turned into."

"It's all theory," she said, "but one of the men was saying they believe a person's mood or humor at the time of their exposure the transformational forces of the planet is the thing that determines his change." Then she laughed. "No, it *can't* be that. You couldn't have been in the mood of a serpent."

"Are you sure?"

I paused and thought the matter over for a moment. I had certainly been spying on Ernest Macklin right up to the moment that the ship began its landing descent. I had been watching him like any sly snake closely watches its prey.

"But *you* couldn't have been a two-headed feline," I continued.

She was amused. "I don't know. When I try to remember that last moment before the ship exploded, all I can recall is that I was very curious—you might say as curious as a cat. I was trying to keep an eye on you and Ernest Macklin at the same time—trying not to displease either of you, though I felt sure that you were almost at swords' points—"

"This theory is sounding a little more credible. Maybe you *were* being a two-headed feline." I chuckled a little with a slight hiss. "If there's anything to it, they'll never find Macklin. It isn't easy to locate a worm, you know."

"But it shouldn't be so hard to pick up a wolf," she said, giving me a quick look. "And I don't mean a harmless wolf either. If it hadn't been for your help on the trip, I think I might have forgot my good manners and shot Ernest Macklin through the heart."

"Really?"

"No...probably not, but I didn't sign up to be his girl friend, you know." She gave me a coy smile. "I've been a friend in need to that little pistol of mine more than once, though."

Then she looked at me sympathetically. "We'll have to get you out of this awful shape. They've made a good start, at least, getting your brain back in order and getting some of your physical human attributes back. But it's just the beginning. Are they going to find a way? Is that what you wanted to share in confidence with me?"

"The confidence I wanted to share with you is that this laboratory seems to be managed by Dr. Hunt."

"Dr. Hunt? *Emerson* Hunt? The one who came here from the Earth? He was rumored to have possibly been forced to come here. You think he's in charge?"

"I believe so. In fact I'm almost certain. It all points that way—these advanced experiments and all. You know what a reputation he had."

"And he's here—still alive?"

"Yes. I'm on his trail."

"You mean—?"

"That's been my 'secret' mission. I've come here to find him. Confidentially, an association of scientists has funded me in a plan to rescue him and bring him back home. You can realize how much it will mean to the Earth—to the whole solar system—if he can be found and convinced to come back."

"Oh!" Flora gasped slightly. "What a boon for Earth that would be...it truly *would* be!"

"If not a boon, at least a blessing."

"Of course..." She became rather excited over this

prospect and her voice raised. I quieted her gently to make sure our conversation wouldn't be overheard by any of the guards. She was at once so enthusiastic that she was ready to break her contract with Macklin simply to help me. Dr. Hunt was one of the most respected scientists of the past century.

"No wonder you were always talking about some big purpose," she said.

"There's a lot I can't tell you yet, but I want you to listen to me carefully. I'm going to need all the help I can get; and I can tell already—I'm sure you can, too—that we're going to be working against this whole weird world. Don't you see that they're thriving here in this strange scientific fortress on the genius of Dr. Hunt? Nobody here is going to let him get away if they can help it. Worst of all, I'm already doubting whether he'll *want* to get away."

"But *why?* If he has a sure chance to get back to the Earth, *why*—"

"Because people change when they come to this land. Dr. Hunt has probably changed too."

"But if you talk to him—if you explain—"

I laughed rather mockingly at her extreme innocence. "Maybe *you* can talk to him...but not me."

"Why not?"

"Look at me...I'm still a serpent. Not an ordinary serpent mind you, but a serpent with four legs and a human mind. To a scientist with the advanced ideas of Dr. Emerson Hunt, I'll be something to be analyzed and observed, maybe even dissected—but certainly not listened to."

"Oh...I see..."

"Eventually, they'll slice me open and see how I'm put together. I've already heard some of the consulting scientists mention that Dr. Hunt will be eager to get my skeleton for his permanent collection."

Suddenly six guards marched in; our visit came to an

abrupt end when they announced that Dr. Hunt was waiting to see me. Flora stood back of her chair, watching speechless as they wheeled me away in my cage.

CHAPTER EIGHT

I HAVE had the common sensation of chills running down my spine many times in normal life, but I must say that I never knew any feeling like this before. When one's spine is fully forty feet long, and a series of chills chases through from head to tail, I'm telling you it's *chilling*.

There was far more to this mountain laboratory than I had guessed at first sight. I hadn't realized that Z Lab could mean just that—the last unit in a series of labs named after the entire alphabet—and after we had moved past six or eight units, each bearing a different letter, I began to get a new appreciation of the extent of the complex.

I soon found out I was on my way to H Laboratory. Possibly Dr. Hunt's favorite lab because it bore his initial?

H Laboratory opened to me automatically. It was an awesome sight. The grilled metal doorway slid back into the wall, and a second door—a checkerboard of silver and gold—parted in the middle and folded backward in two wings.

"No talking now," the guards warned me. I had almost become nebulous to their presence. I was so intent upon the visual detail of all the scientific splendor of the lab.

"No talking," I repeated, rather insolently.

"And no undue crawling or twitching," one of the guards added.

"As if I had room to crawl in this cage," I replied.

"Quiet!" he snapped back at me under his breath.

"I can't even twitch," I added. The serpent instinct was working on me. I was looking for ways to be annoying.

"Can I breathe?"

"All right…just stop talking."

"Hisssss-hisssss!"

"Quiet…"

"I'm just breathing," I said. "Can I help it if I breathe like a serpent?"

The six guards stopped me in the middle of the doorway, put their heads together, and conversed in whispers. I knew I was pushing them a little too far. I half expected them to explode more yellow powder charges over my head to take away more of my serpent attributes.

One of them stalked into a small supply room along the corridor. He returned a moment later bearing something that resembled a long, straight-nosed oil can. I assumed it must be some sort of high-powered hypodermic needle.

I was tempted to pull some fancy whip act and lash the fellow with my tail before he could inject me. Something told me to take it easy, though—there might be worse things in store if I didn't at least *pretend* to cooperate.

They gave me the shot.

The needle pierced my skin about a dozen feet from the tapered end of my body. One sharp, ice-cold jab! All of the chills that had run up and down my spine just minutes before came chasing through again. Chills and dizziness followed, and then…

Ahhhh…

What a sensation of peace. I began to feel tame. Agreeable. Downright happy. All at once I wanted to be the nicest, friendliest serpent that ever went visiting a scientific laboratory.

"That ought to do it," one of the guards murmured.

I turned, touched the brow of my scaled face with my fingers and tried to smile.

"Thank you, gentlemen, I feel much better. What can I do

to return the favor?"

"He's okay now," one of the guards observed. Several of the others nodded in agreement. They proceeded to wheel me into Laboratory H.

I was pleasantly treated to the beauties and mysteries of the most impressive laboratory equipment I had ever seen. The huge glass tubes, standing in clusters above the tables, some nearly thirty feet tall, were illuminated by a battery of colored lights: lavender, light green, purple, deep blue. Their gleaming stems were like frozen music. In one corner of the six-cornered room, a bright orange blur of motion indicated that a governor was spinning silently over a pyramid of shining machinery. One could hear the churning of liquids in the scores of transparent containers that were built into the different levels of the mysterious pyramid, and the orange blur cast its light over the whole series with each revolution. Again, a riot of colors hinted of a mastermind's secrets in blending the molecules of many elements. Who could know what new and rare combinations might come into existence through these experiments?

OUT of the dazzling display I detected one detail that struck me as something not to be forgotten—that yellowish-white powder. At one side of the mixing pyramid I noticed it, sifting down slowly, like sand through an hourglass. Was this not the same sulfur-like substance that had been exploded over my head and earlier dumped over the pool where Flora Hessel had been hiding?

If so, I thought, here might be the source of these scientists' seeming magic.

The nice, kindly feeling that bubbled within me shuddered for just an instant. Then my "serpent slyness" resurfaced for a few moments. *If I could steal some of that powder, what might it do for me? Was this my way back to my human state?*

"The doctor will be in right away," one of the white-uniformed men said. "Is our patient ready to be examined?"

"With pleasure," I said, with as close to a smile as my serpent's face would allow.

The white-uniformed man shot a quick, puzzled look in my direction.

"It's all right, Dr. Winston," a guard said. "We just gave him a shot of Sixty-eight-J-sixty-nine."

Dr. Winston nodded. "Enough to put him to sleep I hope?"

"We're not entirely sure."

Dr. Winston checked a lab slip that the guard showed him and calculated mentally the quantity of the drug they had given me, as compared with my probable blood content. They obviously hadn't had a specimen of my size previously.

"We'll see," Dr. Winston said, nodding again. He then dismissed the guards. A moment later I was left alone with him inside this marvelous laboratory.

My mind was contemplating the situation. So they thought I would go to sleep, did they? Not if I could help it. Still, it gave me an idea.

I spoke drowsily, "Nice place you have here, doctor." I opened my jaws slowly, yawned, and let my eyes go half closed. "Nice place…quiet…restful."

He was watching me out of one corner of his eye as he fiddled with some notes on a clipboard. I seemed to be dropping off into a peaceful slumber—or so he thought. He then went to the telephone.

"Dr. Hunt? Winston here. The four-legged serpent is ready. Obstreperous? Far from it. The attendants gave him a shot of Sixty-eight-J-sixty-nine. He's just fallen asleep."

I allowed my arms to fold on the floor of my cage so that my head and neck sank to the level of my belly. It wasn't a very proud posture—and I must admit it wasn't easy to allow myself to slump into such a dejected-looking heap of flesh—especially in the presence of a fine, kingly looking person like Dr. Winston. He would have looked well in any convention of athletes—broad-shouldered, well-shaped hands, keen gray eyes, and a vigorous head of fine brown hair. He stood with excellent posture, with just enough swagger and toss to his head that it made you think his brain must weigh considerably more than the average man's.

I wondered whether Dr. Hunt would present as perfect an appearance. About all I had remembered of Hunt's picture was the striking black mustache and the sharp-pointed short black beard.

"Hisssssss-hisssssss-hissssss…"

My soft hissing breaths were barely audible. I was sure I had convinced Dr. Winston that I had fallen into a deep slumber. If Dr. Hunt would fall for the ruse, too, I might have a chance to know what the two of them intended to do with me.

Dr. Winston turned at the sound of a slight squeaking from the rear door of lab. Another man entered the room. He rolled into the lab in a luxurious electronically powered chair. Anyone would have known at a glance that the person entering was a high-ranking scientist or official of some sort. Then I recognized who he was. Now that I saw him again, his pictures came back to me—that extremely potent, magnetic quality that strikes out at you from some faces—he had it more than anyone I had ever seen…Emerson Hunt.

There was something about his appearance that I couldn't quite clarify in my reptilian brain. I ignored the troubling thought momentarily and tried hard to keep my eyes on him.

He rolled to a position within a few feet of the front of my cage, and I drank him in—mentally—through the half-slits of my "sleeping" eyes.

He hadn't looked at me too intently yet. The squeak of his

chair annoyed me—and it appeared to be bothering him, too. He reached for the wire-free telephone in the arm of the chair and barked an order to some service department elsewhere in the complex. His physical peculiarity had struck me rather incidentally at first, but now I realized what it was…

He had four arms.

He put down the phone at the same time he mopped the perspiration off his wide brow—at the same time he touched a chair control that moved him a little closer—at the same time his fourth and final hand was reaching into a pocket for another pair of eye-glasses.

The rolling chair had been well designed to accommodate his four-armed body, so much so that one wasn't disturbed by the slight spidery effect of his physical appearance—as long as he remained sitting.

WHEN he rose and began to walk around my cage I was more sensitive to his freakish profusion of appendages. It was all I could do to keep from opening my eyes wide. I was blinking, in spite of myself, but he and Dr. Winston were too busy sizing up my length to notice.

"We'll have to get some measurements, first thing," said Dr. Hunt matter-of-factly. "I'd like to start dissecting as soon as possible."

"You mean within a few hours?" Dr. Winston asked. "It will take at *least* that long to sharpen the knives and gather the instruments needed for a carcass of this magnitude."

Hunt looked briefly at the watch on one of his left wrists. "You understand, of course, why I'm relying upon an early dissection."

Dr. Winston gave an affirmative nod; the two scientists then went into a lengthy discussion of the procedure. I listened closely with mounting trepidation. It was Dr. Hunt's hope that they might be able to produce additional physical specimens like me. He believed that a timely examination of the tissues of my body would show the actual history of my transformation process. These tissues would serve as the biological guides for repeating the experiment.

They talked quietly.

The drug they'd given me had certainly made me drowsy, but I held on to consciousness. I needed to know how soon they were going to cut me into pieces!

A repairman of some sort soon entered the lab. The two scientists dropped their discussion of me in favor of Dr. Hunt's luxurious chair, which appeared to need some form of maintenance.

"Just an oiling job?" the repairman asked. "I'll have it back in a short while."

Dr. Hunt pointed to the brown and blue checkered upholstery, demonstrating its worn places with his four hands. "This upholstery is showing some wear and needs to be replaced."

The repairman nodded and rolled the chair out the front entrance. As soon as he disappeared from view the doctors' discussions returned to me.

"Look…his eyes flickered," said Dr. Winston. "I believe he's awake."

"They tell me he talks," said Dr. Hunt. "Let's have a few words out of him."

Winston turned to me. "Can you say something?"

"Hissssss!" I said loudly.

"Come, come. You can do better than that."

"Hisss. Hisss. Why should I talk if you're going to pick my bones clean and turn me into a laboratory skeleton?"

One of Dr. Hunt's hands raised up and stroked his sharp little beard. He raised his eyebrows and glanced at Dr. Winston.

"I thought you said that they gave him a shot of Sixty-eight-J-sixty-nine?"

"They did," replied Dr. Winston. "He was highly agreeable a few minutes ago."

"I'm highly agreeable now," I said casually, rising to a more comfortable position, straightening my front legs beneath my scaled shoulders. "If you want to start cutting me up right away, *I'll help you sharpen the knives.*"

"Oh, you will?" Dr. Hunt asked in a mildly interested tone. "You *are* being agreeable, aren't you?"

"These front legs of mine are pretty handy," I went on. "I've a good pair of hands on them, as you can see. So I'll help you dissect. I can begin cutting off cross-sections of my tail, if you like…"

"Perhaps the drug's affecting his mind a little more than the usual," Winston commented.

Dr. Hunt was eyeing me closely, not saying a word. I knew that my "cutting" remarks had perplexed him. Perhaps I had gotten under his scientific skin.

"Why don't you boys get smart?" I said disrespectfully.

"Meaning what?" asked Winston.

"Meaning that you're limping along with *old-fashioned methods* in this broken-down lab." I said it with all the conviction I could muster, and it appeared to be driving home. Some of Dr. Hunt's twenty fingers began twitching slightly. I went on digging. "This broken-down lab might be good enough for Space Island, but you couldn't give it away back on the Earth, unless you could find some scientist who's a sucker for antiques."

Dr. Hunt reddened a trifle, then smiled slightly as his two right hands stroked through his ruffled black hair.

"Really?" he asked in a seemingly passive tone. "What kind of equipment do they have on Earth these days that excels the best we have here?"

"They have manufactured a multiple X-ray machine that's

attached to a newly developed plastic molding device. They can turn out a perfect copy of my skeleton—in plastic—without ever touching a knife blade to my skin."

The two doctors exchanged glances.

"The drug has gone to his head," Winston repeated. "I'll get something stronger."

CHAPTER NINE

I'LL never know whether my drugging with Sixty-eight-J-sixty-nine accounted for my actions when the *zeego* guns began to flash all over the place a couple of minutes later.

They say that some men will rise to the greatest heights of bravery, or congeniality, or oratory under the influence of certain beverages, and afterwards they'll wonder whether the achievement was their own or whether it came out of the bottle. That's how it was with me two minutes later when a surprise attack suddenly struck Laboratory H.

It was those damned pygmies!

Wherever they had come from, they were suddenly raiding the complex. The place turned into a madhouse. The flash of *zeego* guns was everywhere. Red fire blasted through the dark corridor, quick sharp lines of it—back and forth and across. Three rays of it cut through the double doors of Laboratory H.

Dr. Winston dropped, and I thought he had been hit. Dr. Hunt spun around, obviously looking for his rolling chair, but it was gone. He strode swiftly across to the nearest lab table and seized a telephone. Before he could speak, five of the three-foot demons were racing in with their guns blazing.

One of them guarded the door while two of them marched over to Dr. Winston, who crouched on the floor, holding his arm as if he was wounded. The other two ran toward Dr. Hunt.

Interestingly enough, they didn't appear to notice me, probably because I was just a specimen in a cage, lying there inert without showing any signs of knowing what was going on. It was a tactical error on their part.

I swung my arm down through an opening between the bars and smacked my hand against the floor. My cage, resting on rollers, lunged forward. Another touch of my hand sent me coasting quickly into the path of the two pygmies who were threatening Dr. Hunt. They were moving fast, but so was I.

They whirled about when they heard me coming. They were completely startled for an instant—you should have seen the look on their faces. However, a moment later they raised their guns and fired. The red fire splashed over the glass sides of my prison. I caught a bit of the spray on my back. I squealed in pain as it struck with the sharpness of a hundred needles. My coiled body snapped like a spring, and my shoulder crashed into the bars with a resounding thud. I drew back, saw the opening I had made, and plunged through.

"Look out! The monster! *Look out!*" one pygmy squealed.

"Monster, huh?" I snarled back as if the word had been one insult too many. I didn't heed their gunfire, though it was piercing through my scaled protection. I leaped at the two of them with both arms swinging. I slammed into one of them. He sailed clear across the room, crashing into a stack of glass tubes while his gun flipped into the air like something flung from a catapult. The second little fellow, obviously stunned with fear at the sight of it all, simply dropped his weapon and backed away, holding his hands behind him.

I pivoted from one arm and whirled my forty-foot length like a whip. That knocked down three of them. A bit of carelessness on my part, though, as the final flash of my tail caught Dr. Winston, who had just come to his feet. So everyone was on the floor except Dr. Hunt and the pygmy who had stayed to guard the door. I went for the guard but he went streaking down the corridor.

The first part of the pygmy attack ended then—at least as far as my direct involvement—as Dr. Hunt touched a switch and the inner door of Laboratory H closed with a loud *Clang!*

So there were seven of us, all locked in securely—and for a moment it was a toss-up as to who would be masters and who would be prisoners. Four pygmies—their brown little bodies adorned with nothing but red loincloths; two doctors—probably the smartest on all of Space Island; and one serpent—a four-legged monstrosity powerful enough to burst out of his cage—and he was out.

In the rage of the moment it seemed that I could have scooped up all of the other persons in the room and choked the life out of them—or at least forced them to my will. But it was not to be. I should have known better than to think that one could defeat a scientist in his own laboratory.

AFTER KNOCKING the one pygmy senseless, I did go so far as to gather up the other three and start toward Dr. Hunt—Dr. Hunt, the man who was planning to strip the flesh from my bones. I'm sure he must have wondered why I troubled to play the hero in his defense. But there was still a certain plan and purpose I had in mind. I still held the dim hope—perhaps foolishly—that I might somehow lift Dr. Hunt out of this strange world and take him home to Earth. It was a pretty fancy ambition for a four-legged serpent.

Dr. Hunt then killed the power to the overhead lights. The place went utterly dark—I stopped in my tracks. Soon my eyes adjusted, though. I could see a single flooding light—dim purple in color—almost like a shower bath of luminous lavender dust. It was coming down over me, illuminating my long six-foot arms, and casting a baleful glow over the three pygmies I held.

I had stopped in my tracks, and suddenly I knew why I had stopped.

The flood of purple light had paralyzed me.

I couldn't move. I was frozen. And the ugly pygmy, over whose waist I had clamped my left hand, was as frozen as I was. The other two, who I had caught by the feet and who hung upside down from my uplifted right arm, never twitched or flicked an eyebrow.

We were all frozen together by some unknown paralysis ray. It was a bit unnerving, even embarrassing. My serpent's jaws were open and my head was inclined toward the pygmy in my left hand. Even in the dim purple light I knew the two doctors would be able to see, plainly enough, what *might* have happened.

I won't say that it *would* have happened, but I will say that the instant the room was plunged in darkness, I must have made a motion as if I were going to eat one of the pygmies— and that was the position in which the paralysis ray had caught me.

"Are you all right, Dr. Winston?" Dr. Hunt called out.

"I'm here," Winston cried back. "That was quick action on your part. You escaped injury, didn't you?"

"Yes…but you were knocked down. I saw you fall."

"The beast's tail caught me. Have you got the paralysis on solid?"

"Solid," said Dr. Hunt. "Another minute and we can put the lights back on. We'd better get a report on the rest of the units in the meanwhile. This attack may be widespread. I've been uneasy about something like this for days."

"Not to worry. The Mashas haven't a chance against us," said Dr. Winston in a stout voice. "This little flare-up can't last long. They tried before, you know."

"They've been trying for 150 years," said Dr. Hunt. "I've

studied the records of this facility, and I've found that troubles like these have recurred every ten or fifteen years."

Dr. Hunt got through to his various subordinates on the telephone. He talked in an agitated manner at first until their reassurances calmed him. The attack had come and gone like a quick thundershower. He hung up, satisfied that the complex was in no serious danger. A moment later he turned on the lights and opened the laboratory doors, all the while reporting the situation to Dr. Winston.

"They've captured fifteen of the troublemakers—none of them were identified as our servants. In fact, I'm glad to say there hasn't been any uprising at all among our servants. That means that our serums are still working."

"Then the only trouble came from outsiders?" Winston asked.

"Apparently."

Winston shook his head at this. "You know, if it had been our own servants—who admittedly are under forced labor—I could have understood the reason for the uprising. But what I can't understand is why the Mashas who live on the outside, who have the whole countryside to live in, and who haven't been enslaved in any way, should take it upon themselves to storm our fortress."

"I don't fully understand it, either, but I'm sure it at least has something to do with 'liberating' our servants." Dr. Hunt admitted slowly. He stroked his sharp black beard thoughtfully. "I wish we had some way of getting into the mind of a Masha. If we could just find out what they're planning."

They sauntered back in my direction, and then, as if with a single inspiration, they stopped and stared at me. They gazed at the three unmoving Mashas in my grasp.

"I wonder," Dr. Hunt said slowly.

"I was thinking same thing," said Dr. Winston. "Maybe

we *do* have a way of finding out—a decidedly ingenious way."

Dr. Hunt looked me over carefully, giving particular attention to my open jaws. The Mashas were doubly frozen—once from the paralysis ray and once from fear.

"I'd hate like sin to let one of the finest specimens we've ever created get away. But I'd risk a lot to find out more about the Mashas that live on the outside. They may someday pose a serious threat to us—in spite of our technological advantages."

He reached over and put a hand on the side of my paralyzed cheek. A wry smile came across his face.

Yes, I think it might be worth a try," said Dr. Hunt.

CHAPTER TEN

You never saw such tender care exercised upon a serpent. They fed me the most wonderful foods and gave me the most comfortable bed I could ask for. They treated my wounds with a dozen kinds of salves and oils; they bathed and massaged me and manicured me; they took me out for exercise, allowing me to run along at my own pace, hitched by a rope to a ten-ton truck.

It was wonderful while it lasted. I was their favorite pet dog, you might say, and they considered it a privilege to walk me.

The only trouble with the exercise periods was that they always occurred at night, so that I didn't have much chance to study the countryside. That was their precaution. They also didn't want the outside pygmies—the Mashas—to know that they were grooming me for a special purpose.

Best of all, they gave me access to an indoor swimming pool where I could thrash around and whip the water about to my tail's content.

"Is everything perfectly satisfactory?" the attendants

would ask me. "Is the water the right temperature? You *don't* care for a towel, do you? If so, don't hesitate to let us know."

"Ah...er...I was thinking of one thing in particular," I said, recalling those first strange hours down in the stream in the bottom of the crevasse. "I have a weakness for blossom-scented air. Could you arrange to have some flowers brought in and placed beside the pool?"

When Flora Hessel came to visit me in my room, and I described all of my luxuries to her, she was not as surprised as I had expected.

"It's no more than you deserve," she said. "After all, you saved the lives of the two most important men in this kingdom."

"I did?"

"Oh, you needn't be so modest about it. Everyone has heard by this time. That little band of Mashas was all set to take over the fortress from the inside. If they had captured Laboratory H, as they planned, they could have given orders from Dr. Hunt's control phones. There'd have been countless Mashas pouring in from all directions before the scheme was discovered."

I shook my head slowly. "Now I'm not trying to argue for the sake of argument, and if these rumors are making the rounds, I suppose there must be some basis for them. But tell me this, how could any pygmy—or Masha I mean—imitate Dr. Hunt over the phone?"

"I don't know," she said. "Perhaps they have certain vocal abilities we aren't aware of."

"But a pygmy imitating Dr. Hunt—that would be like a mouse imitating a lion. Have you heard Dr. Hunt's big solid voice? It's deep, it's throaty, it's full of chesty thunder. Have you heard any of these pygmy servants speak? It's not even close."

She shrugged her shoulders. "Regardless, you saved a

couple of important lives."

I bloated up my snakely chest with pride, but this went unnoticed by Flora. She was looking out the window at the green ridge of mountains in the distance, deep in thought. I wondered if my point about the disparity between pygmy and human voices had given her pause.

"You know," she said presently, "I think you've got a valid point. Perhaps the pygmies weren't going to use a *pygmy* to imitate Dr. Hunt." She turned and looked directly at me, a somewhat concerned look on her face. "Maybe they were going to use someone from the inside, someone from here at the fortress—one of the guards—one of Dr. Hunt's secretaries—perhaps even one of the doctors."

"Hmmm," I responded. It was a tantalizing thought.

"There could be a traitor," she continued.

"But who?"

"I don't know…but there was only one other person in the lab with Dr. Hunt at the time of the attack. Maybe this Dr. Winston you told me about was all set to step into Dr. Hunt's shoes, using the little people as his army," Flora went on, now looking farther into the distance.

"No, no, it couldn't be that," I responded. "It's like Dr. Hunt said, all you have to do is consult the record to see that the Mashas have been bursting out with an attack every ten or fifteen years."

The Mashas were the original outcasts from Mars. Their original name, "Martians," had degenerated into the word Mashas. Their physical characteristics had been warped and changed from their original man-like stature to the small, wiry, shrunken bodies they now possessed. It had happened during their first fifty years on Mars. The scientific reason was unclear, but it was theorized that exposure to an unknown radiation from an ancient meteorite near the area of their original settlement, had caused the change. Mars had "marshed" them, as the phrase had originally been coined; later, it was said to have "mashed" them, thus, the evolution of the word, "Masha." Incredibly, the physical change had also been accompanied with a prolongment of physical life. They were all about two hundred years old and they had seemed largely impervious to the transformation process that afflicted so many other life forms on Space Island. How much longer they would live, no one knew. They were one of the true scientific oddities of the galaxy.

The later generations of Martian settlers, who held the "Mashas" in utter contempt, had brutally exiled them into deep space. Here they were, though, still alive and kicking, and still rankling from the mistreatment of a hundred and fifty years ago.

"One can't help feeling sorry over their plight," Flora said philosophically. "It's all a trick of fate."

"It's been done, and it can't be undone," I said. "For all we know, they may live on another couple of centuries—or hell, they may make trouble for a thousand years, who knows. This freakish planet might refuse to let them die."

"Well, they *can* die, you know," said Flora, giving me a quick eye. "You've already accounted for the subject; I went into detail about the events regarding my "rescue" of Dr. Hunt in Laboratory H. I went over in fine detail everything that had happened, including being frozen by the paralysis ray just as I appeared ready to take a bite out of one of the pygmies.

"Everything that happened showed the doctors two specific things," I said. "One, my tough scales can withstand a certain amount of *zeego* fire. Two, my tough stomach is good for at least a limited quantity of pygmy steak."

"I could have told them that," Flora said with a slight grin.

"Well, there you have it. That's the reason they're treating me to all these luxuries."

"You mean it isn't because you're a hero?"

"Heroes get banquets and medals and speeches. That's because their work is already done. But these boys are grooming me for a *new job*—a big job that's never been done before. They're virtually bribing me to do it well." I then told her about the plans they had for me regarding the Mashas.

Flora gave out a long "Hmmm." She seemed somewhat disturbed.

"Just where does this get you in relation to your own purpose?" She asked. "When you get through exploring the inside of the Masha world as a favor to Dr. Hunt, is he going to pack up and go back to the Earth as a favor to you?"

I couldn't answer that in the affirmative and be truthful. And in Flora's presence I didn't feel like being a lying snake. So I simply didn't answer.

She walked to the door, and just before she walked away she gave her own answer.

"The first chance you get," she said, "take a walk down the spiral passage beyond Laboratory X and you'll come to the Dr. Hunt's Museum of Skeletons. You'll find your answer there."

She seemed to be saying, "Walk into their trap, you stupid fool," though she hadn't used those exact words.

"Just a minute, there," I called out to her. "How did *you* happen to find your way down into the Museum of Skeletons? I'm barred from that area of the complex, and most of the labs, too. Besides, I thought you were more-or-less a prisoner here. Or are you more of a tourist? Or are you asking for a job feeding the skeletons?"

She tossed her dark hair over her shoulders and flashed her dark eyes at me. "I guess it wouldn't make any difference if I *did* tell you."

"I've got tough scales. I think I can take it," I shot back.

"All right. I went down there because I had a date with a charming wolf in sheep's clothing. I'm going back again tomorrow night, too."

CHAPTER ELEVEN

I MUST have been pretty desperate to take the chance I took the very next night. I was desperate. I was boiling with an inner rage that was born not of fear but of jealousy.

"Take me *that* way," I said to the attendant who was examining the hitch at the end of my exercise truck. "Take me back into the mountain road that curves over the buildings."

The attendant shrugged as if it made no difference to him, so long as I got my exercise. He went up front and crawled in beside the driver. Neither he nor the driver guessed what was in my mind. They were finding me a cooperative pet who could be led to water, and that was all they cared.

I couldn't help wondering whether a pygmy driver would have been as unconcerned. But the authorities had their eye on that, too. They knew there might be a leak of information from the fortress to the outside Mashas, and if so, that leak was probably one of the trusted little Masha slaves who, in spite of the doctor's regular doses of serum, contained a spark of rebellious thought.

The pygmy servants had all come under close watch in recent days. If one of them should be found to have helped with the recent attack, they would no doubt be treated to something pretty severe. More serum, perhaps? Torture or death? It was anybody's guess. The scientists were playing a bold game. If only one could only get inside the mind of Dr. Emerson Hunt.

As I began running alongside the truck, my thoughts turned again to the Mashas. The strange little creatures were tougher than most newcomers to Space Island. Their training period in Mars over a century ago had stiffened their resistance to the capricious forces of this planet, forces that turned all manner of men into all manner of freaks. Yet still, the scientists' serums were able to effect *temporary* differences in their week-to-week behavior. As long as they were continuously drugged they made excellent slaves—dull, obedient, dependable, and as a rule, non-vicious.

My mind was reeling with a myriad of notions as I increased the speed of my running, the noise of the truck almost drowning out my thoughts.

There was the problem of the wild transformations of the more recent arrivals from Earth. These persons had come to Space Island, arriving—in many cases—transformed. But why? And how? One could only hope that the brilliant scientists from Dr. Hunt's laboratories could answer such questions. For my part, I stood as living proof that such things *did* happen. I had also seen the retransformation process take place—completely in the case of Flora Hessel, and partially in my own case.

"What of Dr. Hunt's arms?" I wondered aloud, breathing heavily as I ran on and on. Had this been an accidental transformation…or a *controlled* transformation?

One thing appeared certain, though—Emerson Hunt *wanted* those four arms. He had use for all of them, and they did much to increase his efficiency. *If* he had wanted a completely normal body, wouldn't he have applied the yellow powders that had been used on Flora and later on me? Certainly they would have caused a quick and massive change in nature's delicate arrangement of his biological parts…

It was no wonder that I, the serpent victim of this ungodly freak factory, was losing sleep trying to understand all the forces and schemes in play on this lonely planet. Here I was, the only human serpent—the only four-legged serpent with human hands and a human brain! In all of Space Island there was not another like me.

But yet there *were* men—ever so many normal men—like Dr. Winston and the attendants and guards. And there were at least a few women. Had all of them come through some violent transformation and retransformation, the same as Flora Hessel?

Ah, now *there* was a woman. As I ran alongside the truck this was at once the most hopeful and yet most disturbing thought of all.

Flora!

I knew that there wasn't another person on the planet who was so much a friend to me as Flora Hessel. Of all the brilliant persons who had observed me and questioned me and cared for me, she was the only one who had said, *"You must get out of this form. You must get yourself back to your normal state."*

And then I came back to the feverish, jealous thoughts that had caused me to ask the attendant to take me over this particular section of road.

Jealousy? Or was it something less definite? Suspicion? Perhaps that was it. Flora had had a date with a *charming wolf in sheep's clothing*, she had said. That could mean only one thing I thought...

Ernest Macklin.

He was still alive. He was somewhere in the immediate vicinity, and he had seen Flora.

I didn't like it. I remembered what she had said about relying upon my protection during our space hop. Otherwise, she had said, she might have resorted to the use of her pistol.

Did she have a pistol now?

How had he found her? Where had they met? Why had she agreed to go with him through the spiral tunnel beyond Laboratory X to explore a museum full of bones? Before the night's exercise was over I meant to find some of the answers.

I had only the vaguest idea, admittedly, as to how much exercise would be required before I got to my destination. The truck had swung around the wide plaza and taken a cloverleaf turn to ascend the mountain road. I figured we were moving at close to ten miles an hour. The rope they had fastened to the harness around my neck and shoulders was long enough that I could run up alongside the cab to check on my speed.

"How fast?" I asked.

The attendant and the driver both gave a nervous lurch whenever they saw me moving along outside their window.

"Eight miles an hour," said the attendant. "Take it easy. You're not supposed to overwork."

"I feel like going faster," I said. I stepped up my speed and would have run along in front of them if they hadn't stepped on the accelerator. I don't think they liked the sight of me moving along in their lights. After all, I must have looked to them like the world's biggest, snakiest lizard, galloping along on a leash.

They moved past me, but I soon caught up again.

"Step on it," I said. "I need the exercise."

They doubled their pace, but I stayed with them.

In a few moments the attendant called out to me, "We're up to thirty-two miles an hour. That's fast enough. They'll give me hell if I let you run your legs off."

"It's a perfectly comfortable speed," I said. "But I'm in the mood to race."

"Oh...so that's it." The attendant growled something to the driver and the truck sped up.

I KEPT an eye on the road as we accelerated again. I was kicking up my share of dust now as we hit forty-five miles an hour. Every now and then my tail would whip down against the road, unintentionally of course. It was a beginner's awkwardness, you might say. No snake spanks himself on purpose.

I was watching the road closely. Soon came the long section I had been waiting for. It was a good piece of road except that it was full of twists and turns, which were somewhat jarring to a serpent's backbone. Just below the edge of the road the ledge dropped straight down about sixty feet—to the roofs of the fortress. We were now higher than the laboratories themselves.

I bounded up beside the cab and shouted, "Faster!"

The driver moved the speedometer up to sixty-five miles an hour. "How's that?" he yelled.

"Just right," I said, falling back gradually. "Hold it right there for ten minutes."

"Can you take it?"

"If I can't, I'll shout."

I then fell back gradually. The driver and the attendant kept their spotlight on the curves ahead and left me to myself. That was just what I wanted.

Snap!

I had been biting at the rope that was fastened to my harness for several miles. With one savage bite I finished the job. I was free.

The truck whirled on around a bend, dragging the rope behind it.

I bounded down over the embankment, clinging tight with all of my crawling muscles. Four or five minutes later, when the sounds of the truck's brakes reached my ears, I was already slithering over the glass and metal roofs of the laboratories. I was in the mood to be free for a change, and it would take more than six moons and a truck's spotlight to find me among these roofs.

CHAPTER TWELVE

I RESTED for a full hour, lying in a hiding place a few feet from a chimney and a ventilator. I could imagine what the driver and the attendant were saying as they played their spotlight over the rocks, up and down the mountainside and out across the roofs, looking for me. They would need to practice their story well before they went back empty handed.

I could just hear them trying to pass the buck. "I *told* the driver we shouldn't race him faster than fifteen miles an hour." Or perhaps, "How the hell did *I* know? I'm just the driver, and if the damned snake wanted exercise, it made no difference to me what speed we were going, as long as the attendant didn't mind."

But I knew none of their alibis would be good enough—unless of course they could produce the serpent. The crusty old Captain of the Guards would probably get the job of running me down. I knew he was the kind of man who would make a thorough job of it, too. I had to get going before they got the search squads on my trail.

As soon as the flashes of light ceased to glide over the roofs, I took a chance and crawled quietly to the nearest dimly lit section of glass roof.

"A greenhouse," I said to myself. "Now where would the laboratories be from here?"

I lumbered along at a good pace over the metal surfaces. Their rust and grime and rock dust didn't make for comfortable crawling. Over the glass roofs I took extra care. Once I struck a loose pane and it fell through with a crash. Another light came on, down in that section of greenhouse, and a pygmy gardener came in with a sprinkler in his hand, looking around to see what was the matter.

I tried to hold my breath. When I let go with a quiet

"Hssssh!" he looked up and saw my head through the aperture. He screeched bloody murder and rolled over his sprinkler in a faint. I had no intention of waiting around for him to revive, so I skimmed along to a safer area. At least, I hoped it would be a safer area. But the direction I chose failed to offer the solitude I needed as I came to a sudden stop...

Eight pygmies on the roof!

Now what were *they* doing here? The most obvious answer was they were up to no good. I crawled up silently and peered in on them.

Down in a four-foot depression where the irregular roofs had been joined with a patchwork of corrugated metal, they had lit several torches and were heating up a branding iron.

"Put your initials on him while you're at it," one of them said, adding a low, cackling laugh.

"Don't let him squeal and spoil the fun," came another Masha cackle.

One of the dark little creatures waved a restraining hand across the firelight. "Before we touch the iron, he might like to have one more chance. How about it, Kipper?"

It was seven against one. I crept a little closer to study the evil faces by the light of the torches. Eight little Mashas. Seven of them wore only the red loincloths, the costume of the outsider.

The eighth wore, in addition to the red loincloth, a green neckband, which was the band of a servant, and an armband, which denoted his particular rank and function. He was tied and gagged, completely helpless as a mouse caught in a trap.

The leader of the seven outsiders swung the red-hot iron in a circle. "Anything to say, Kipper? Wouldn't you like to play on our side for a change?"

"Wug!" That was all he could say, choked by a cloth gag.

"Touch him up with the heat and he'll whistle out of his

ears. Here, give *me* the iron—"

But the leader motioned the other pygmy to move back. Then he looked at their prisoner. "We've found out about you, Kipper. We've found out that you're not really one of their slaves. You're playing the part of a servant all right, but you're also playing some game of your own. Now you're going to tell us all about it. We'll even give you a chance to come back to us—but you *will* talk…"

Kipper's eyes were stubborn slits, and his wrinkled brown cheeks were as hard as steel. There was a defiance in his little jaws that his seven torturers weren't going to break down.

"All right, Kipper…have it your way."

The leader ran the point of the red-hot iron lightly across his chest to burn a thin dark line. Kipper's elbows dug tight at his sides.

The leader withdrew the iron. The dim light showed the gleam of cruelty in his round eyes. His large mouth sagged with a brutal expression. You could almost hear the clank of chains in his thin, taunting voice. The leader's name was Jallan, one of the plotters who had engineered the recent attack on the fortress.

"Now, my friend," Jallan said as he snatched the gag out of Kipper's mouth, "we give you your last chance. Are you willing to give us the information we want? Are you willing to come along and help us gain back control of our planet? Are you willing? Or are you going to go on another hundred years being a lone wolf?"

"I was a lone wolf on Mars," said Kipper coldly. "I've never asked a damned thing of any of you except that you let me go my own way."

Jallan gave a flourish with the iron. He touched the point of it to the torches that burned together in a single red flame.

"Put the gag in his mouth, Padderman. Or should we let his scream make music for the whole valley of Mashas?"

One of the pygmies stepped forward and reinserted the gag.

"That's it, gag him well. Now we'll give him something he'll carry with him for a thousand years."

"Brand him with an 'LW' for lone wolf," said Padderman, marking the letters in the night air with his gnarled finger.

"I'll brand a hole right through to his insides. Here we go, Kipper…"

"Hissssss!" I breathed audibly. Then more forcibly. *"HISSSSSSSSS!"*

The second blast from my serpent lips upset the party and blew their fire out.

"Serpent!" someone cried. They all saw me, looming there above them. That was more than enough to send them scampering like bats out of hell. The beating of their feet over tin roofs caused a huge racket. Off into the distance of the night they scattered.

When the sounds of their disorganized retreat had died away, there was still the low hissing of my breath and the sizzle of my spit on the red-hot branding iron. And there was still the muffled choking, gasping, and coughing of Kipper as I drew the gag out of his mouth and unfastened the cords that bound him.

"Don't be afraid of me," I said, as gently as any serpent could be expected to speak under the circumstances. "I had a square meal earlier in the evening. I'll not be dangerous."

CHAPTER THIRTEEN

IT WAS a strange friendship that grew out of that meeting. If I ever met a bold and hardy spirit, Kipper was it. The old term, Lone Wolf, had never meant much to me before. But here was a man who definitely fit the description.

A *man*, did I say?

For the first time, I was thinking of a pygmy not in terms of the calories he would offer my hungry stomach, but in terms of the staunch, stubborn, indomitable human will that characterizes a man.

Here was a two-and-a-half-foot human creature who had cut his own pattern of life for more than two centuries. The rigors of severe Martian winters and the magic of that baffling climate had taken a toll. He no longer possessed the proud five-foot-ten stature that had been his original earthly appearance. But shrunken and dwarfed and wrinkled and ancient, he was still a man who possessed his own will.

Before the night was an hour older, he was telling me, as confidentially as a brother, how he came and went through the halls of Dr. Hunt's scientific fortress.

"A servant? Yes, I'm a servant. I'm a servant because I want to be, not because the serums force me to be."

"But they do give you the serums?" I asked.

"Like clockwork. But I *resist* the effects. Don't ask me how. That's just me. I resist the effects of medicine the same as I resist the influences of my enemies. Sometimes I pay a price."

He touched the burn across his chest.

THE SQUADRON from the Captain's headquarters was moving along the mountain road above the buildings' roofs now, playing their searchlights in all directions. The scampering Mashas were probably getting a second scare, unless they had a very safe hiding place near the fortress.

"We'll be safer down in the laboratories," Kipper said. "Or do you dare go down?"

"That's exactly what I want to do."

"Good. There's an open skylight over this way. It's my regular night exit when I need a breath of air—and incidentally, it's a favorite entrance for the Mashas who have

65

designs on this realm."

"Lead the way," I said.

Kipper led me toward the skylight. For him it was a well-worn trail. For me it was full of hazards—openings that were too small and glass walls that were too fragile for my weight. However, twenty minutes of twisting and turning and feeling our way through dark passages, brought us to a deep basement descent, dimly illuminated with blue wall lights.

"This," said Kipper, "spirals down to the Museum of Skeletons. I'll go down with you."

"Just a minute," I said, suddenly feeling a little awkward. While I had certainly set out to find a way into the labs from above, I wasn't sure I wanted company when I got there. Laboratory X had been my specific goal, with its spiral passage beyond, and eventually the Museum of Skeletons. I looked at him somewhat sheepishly and continued, "I hope you'll pardon me if I meet a friend down there."

"That's *my* expectation," said Kipper, a surprised look on his face. "I intend to meet a friend as well."

"What?" I was growing somewhat ill at ease. If I did run into Flora and Ernest Macklin, I didn't want other people around. "Perhaps I better explain myself," I continued. "I have a friend. A lovely lady named Flora…Flora Hessel. I also have…well…an enemy of sorts. 'Adversary' might be a better word. Flora herself described him as a wolf in sheep's clothing. The less they see of each other, the better it suits me. But she told me very bluntly that she had met him down here just recently and planned on meeting him again tonight. Do you follow my drift?"

"Go on," said Kipper.

"What can I say? I like the gal," I said. "Even though I'm now living a serpent-like existence, someday—hopefully soon—I'm going to return to normal, and when I do she'll be seeing a great deal more of me. At any rate, I hate to see her get mixed up with a hard-boiled wolf like Ernest Macklin. He just isn't good for her, believe me."

"This wolf's name is Ernest Macklin?" Kipper asked.

"Yes."

"So you're jealous."

"Well what do you expect? I'm a green-eyed serpent. That's why I've come. If I find that he's lurking around down there, I'm going to have the pleasure of snapping his head off before I report back to headquarters."

KIPPER was looking at me with a curious look on his face. Suddenly, though, his expression changed. He cupped his ear. I thought I heard it, too…

Footsteps.

It might be Flora coming down our way, or perhaps Macklin. I wondered if I had divulged too much to him. He was beginning to smile at me strangely.

"I hope I'm not in danger," Kipper said.

"Why should you be?"

"Didn't you say she had a date with a wolf?"

"Yes but—"

"All right, I have a date, too."

"With who?"

He paused for a moment, the slightest hint of a grin on his face.

"With Flora Hessel," said Kipper. "I must be the wolf she referred to."

I blinked with complete surprise. Had I misjudged this keen-eyed, straight-shooting little fellow? "You—a wolf?"

"Didn't you hear them call me a Lone Wolf? They were even going to brand me with an L.W. I think that's probably what Flora meant when she described me as a wolf."

"So she meant *you?*"

By that time the footsteps rounded a corner and Flora

suddenly stepped into view. She gave a surprised gasp to see the two of us together.

"Good heavens!" she cried. She looked at me first, then at Kipper. "The two of you know each other?" There was almost a touch of delight in her voice.

"It would appear so," Kipper said dryly.

"Hi, Flora," I added sheepishly.

"That—that's just fine," she stammered. "Well...it *is* fine. In fact, I'm really quite glad about it." She smiled and looked in my direction. "Isn't he charming, Bob? I told you he was a charming wolf in sheep's clothing, didn't I?"

Kipper cleared his throat. "*Lone* Wolf, if you please. You mixed your terms, Madam, and I think you'd better apologize before your misshapen friend gets the wrong impression about us."

"Oh...I'm sorry. *Lone* wolf, of course. Anyway, Bob, our friend Kipper here is a perfectly delightful gentleman, and he's given me more information about the goings-on of this place than I'd get from the attendants in a hundred years. He's helped me immeasurably since I arrived..."

She talked on, as glibly as a chattering magpie. Moments later she and Kipper were leading me into the opening chamber of the Museum of Skeletons. All of my jealous emotions were suddenly gone. If I failed to catch all the interesting facts they were giving me as they guided me along, it was because I was saying to myself, "What a silly serpent you were, Bob Garrison, to get all green-eyed about nothing at all. It was your foolish imagination."

And yet I couldn't reprimand myself too much. Had my jealousy not dictated the evening's chain of events, I wouldn't have saved Kipper from an ugly, possibly fatal ordeal. As it was, I knew I now had not one, but two friends—and both seemed wise and understanding.

"But Flora," I broke in, "I'm still in the dark about Ernest

Macklin. Hasn't he popped up anywhere along the line to claim your services?"

She shook her pretty head. "I haven't seen him since we came into the planet's explosion zone," she said.

Kipper had stopped to listen at one of the museum phones, which he quietly placed to his ear.

"A bit of trouble back in the laboratories," he said. "They're all stirred up over their missing serpent."

"I should probably go back and report in," I said.

"That would be safest," said Kipper. "Otherwise they may punish the driver and the attendant severely for losing you."

"I'll have to go back over the rooftops. They can't know I've been in here."

"That's probably the wisest thing to do. I'll go with you and show you some shortcuts."

"Thanks."

"Besides," he added with a sarcastic grin. They might even send out a general announcement to shoot you on sight."

"Point well taken," I said. I took a quick look at the weird conglomeration of skeletal forms all around me, gleaming white and chalky in the blue light. There was one pedestal that had been placed recently, with no skeleton on it.

I looked at Flora. "This was what you wanted me to see, wasn't it?"

Flora gave me a quick nod. We both knew it was being prepared for me. We hurried away without speaking of it. I was filling up with unanswered questions again.

"Worried?" Kipper asked blithely as we made our exit.

"It's nothing," I said. "Just a slight ache through my vertebrae."

CHAPTER FOURTEEN

WITH Kipper's help, Flora returned to the elevation of general living quarters unnoticed. He assisted me in slipping over the rooftops and down to a side ground-level entrance into a corridor that would lead to Laboratory H—Dr. Hunt's own stomping ground and one of the few labs I was normally granted free access to.

"You don't jump through walls, and they know it," Kipper advised me before he left, "so you'd better get some answers ready for them. But don't tell them too much. Remember, you're a snake."

"Hissss!" I said agreeably.

Kipper gave me a satisfied wink and went on his way.

I knew how to put a stop to all of the quandary over my disappearance. I'd simply go to the phone from which Dr. Hunt made his general announcements, then call up the operator in my living quarters section and say, "Hissss! When do I get my ssssupper?" Then I'd explain that my rope had snapped while running at such a high speed and that I'd made my way back to the complex on foot, taking my time as I did. I'd tell them I'd entered unnoticed through a side entrance, which was actually true.

I was crossing through the six-cornered room, moving carefully and silently, for it was pretty much completely black inside, and I didn't want to welcome myself back with a crash of any expensive glass tubes. I needed to find a light switch. I had gotten as far as Dr. Hunt's rolling chair in the middle of the room when I heard the sound of low voices from somewhere near a lab table over to one side. I squatted down as best I could.

One of the voices was that of Dr. Winston.

"How much do you think the serpent knows?" Winston

asked quietly.

I could see Winston's tall, courtly figure silhouetted against the faint circle of light emanating from one of the instruments next to the table.

The voice that answered Winston was not familiar, but I knew at once that it was not Dr. Hunt's. It had a deep-cistern quality—a hollow echo, like a voice coming through a long, dark tunnel. And yet it was distinct, with sharp, crackling edges to the consonant sounds, like little crackles of thunder very close to your ear.

"He knows," said the deep-cistern voice, "that Dr. Hunt was forced to come here."

"Then he may also know," said Dr. Winston, "that there *is* a power that holds Dr. Hunt in control."

"I don't think so. The serpent has not seen me," said the deep-cistern voice.

"I thought," Winston said, "that you had succeeded in influencing Dr. Hunt to having the serpent killed for his skeleton…for the museum?"

"That has been my intention," the voice rumbled. "But after the Masha attack, Hunt's own plan became paramount in his mind, in spite of my efforts. A man as mentally strong as Emerson Hunt is never completely subordinated…"

I was getting an earful. I tried to catch sight of the man with the deep-cistern tones, but he appeared to be standing on the other side of the table; and try as I may, I couldn't see anyone except Dr. Winston. I was taking an awful risk just being here. My nerves were taut and my tail kept twitching.

What if they should turn on a light?

What a dilemma. Somewhere there were officials stewing over my disappearance. The driver and the attendant were probably getting a verbal roasting for their carelessness. I needed to find Dr. Hunt at once and prove that I had come back unharmed. But I couldn't—at least not for the moment.

Here, in one quick earful, I'd learned more about Dr. Hunt and Dr. Winston than at any time since my arrival at Space Island.

NOW I saw plainly that someone held at least a limited form of mental power over Dr. Hunt. Perhaps he wasn't even aware of which thoughts were his own, and which weren't. It was that power that had initially prompted him to dissect me. Yet it was Hunt's own will that had caused the postponement of that decision. Regardless, I felt certain the power that controlled Emerson Hunt came from the person with the deep-cistern voice.

And what of Winston? Winston—the fine, handsome hero with the suave manner and the kingly appearance. Was Winston also in league with this superior agent? Were the two of them keeping Dr. Hunt under their control? For what purpose?

"Using him as a puppet," I thought.

Yet, Dr. Hunt had delayed my dissection out of his own decision to send me on a mission—to let me confront the skulking outcasts of space who called themselves the Mashas, to see whether I could learn, from the inside, what dangerous powers they possessed and what their plans were.

But hadn't Dr. Winston also had the same idea?

As I looked back at the chain of events during the attack on the lab, it seemed to me that both doctors had come up with the same idea more-or-less at the same moment. It had happened under the purple light of the paralysis ray, when I had stood frozen with three pygmies beneath my open jaws. I wondered...

Suddenly Dr. Winston's blackened image moved across the room toward another lab table. I tensed in anticipation of a light switch going on. I didn't dare creep any further into the room. I might bump into the deep voiced figure, whom I still couldn't see. Should I back away and hide or should I face them? After what I had just heard, I knew there was a chance they would kill me...

I was squatting next to Dr. Hunt's power-chair. The chair was actually quite large and was in many ways more like a miniature truck with an open cab. I crawled silently in back and into the underside of it. The low noises and hums from some of the lab equipment hid the sound of my movements.

I did a good job of coiling myself up inside of it, but quite a length of my tail was left over. This, however, I coiled into a disc of flesh and folded up and over into the seat. I was hidden about as well as my size permitted.

The lights suddenly went on along one wall.

I thought I caught a glimpse of the deep-cistern voice for just an instant, at the edge of the green glow. But I was uncertain of what I saw. From the corner of my eye it seemed that I saw *a huge, ghostly white human skull, triple the size of a normal human head.* It moved back out of my range of vision, and I didn't dare rise up and look.

"I should go," the voice said. "Dr. Hunt shouldn't find us here together."

"He'll be in soon," said Winston. "Right now he's holding a disciplinary session for the two men who let the serpent get away. As soon as he calls, I'll send his chair in for him."

The deep voice chuckled. "Very fond of that throne, isn't he? Why don't you take that honor away from him?"

I SHUDDERED at the thought of Winston actually driving the chair. Chills circled through my coiled body. I remained completely motionless.

"You're tempting me," said Dr. Winston. I could see him standing a few feet in front of the chair, stroking his square jaw with his white, sensitive fingers.

"You might consider allowing yourself four arms, too, you

know," said the deep-voiced person. "Then you'd fit into that rolling throne quite as gracefully as he does."

"I can fit into it anyway," Winston said, not sure that he was being taunted. He was looking at me without seeing me. The color of my green and purples scales blended in perfectly with the color of the upholstery. I felt like a chameleon. But the color effect seemed to make an impression.

"Well, look at this..." said Winston.

"What?"

"New upholstery job. Hunt's been asking for it. But I hadn't noticed—"

The phone on the chair gave two sharp rings.

"That's Hunt, calling for me," Winston said. "I might as well drive it in myself."

He crawled into the seat and leaned back against the flattened coils of my flesh. I was petrified.

I was sure the deep-voiced person would have seen me at that moment. But I was wrong. He spoke, "Well, how does it feel? Quite important, eh? You'd like it, Winston. Think it over."

The phone rang again—two angry rings.

Dr. Winston touched the controls. The rolling chair gave a little lurch, then stopped short. I must have been weighing down on the brakes. I tried to shift just a trifle.

Two more rings.

"Better get going," the voice called from the far side of the room. "He'll be suspicious."

"I'm *trying*—"

"Well, anyway, *I'm* going. Think over what I told you."

The swishing of his receding footsteps gave me the picture of large, soft-surfaced feet beneath a body that carried a huge human skull. The mysterious man—or creature—who directed the sinister goings-on in these laboratories was making a quiet exit. I leaned, trying to catch one more glimpse; but my effort seemed to be too much for the balance of the chair. As it began to tip, I saw the disappearing shadow of a massive skull, with light from an outer room gleaming through a translucent eye. Then the rear door closed.

The chair was tipping backwards. I touched my hand to the floor just in time to avoid a spill.

"Oooof!"

Dr. Winston jerked forward.

"What the…"

Then he sat back, testing the seat. He bounced a little, and was about to get out to see what was wrong; but the coils of my tail moved just a trifle. I knew I was caught. But he pushed the "upholstery" back and brushed his hands, muttering, "Sticky…"

Dr. Hunt then came striding in through the lab doors, looking somewhat exasperated.

"What's the matter? Why didn't you send the chair in?" Hunt stopped short, giving Winston the cold eye. "What's going on? Trading places with me are you?"

"Something's wrong," said Winston weakly. "I couldn't get it to go."

"Get off. I'll show you how."

"It's like I'm stuck in the new upholstery," said Winston.

"*New* upholstery? *What* new—*Ugh! Good heavens!*"

The doctor's eyes widened in a way that caused Winston's mouth to drop open. Or perhaps it was because I had decided to uncurl myself. I uncurled rapidly, but the curve of my tail slid into a loop around Dr. Winston's waist. I drew him right over the back of the chair. He gave a gulping sound and started to mutter some sort of prayer under his breath. A moment later he got a good look at me and fainted dead away.

I dropped his limp body to the floor and turned to drink

in Dr. Hunt's frozen stare. I glanced upward for a moment, thinking that the paralysis ray must be on. No—it was simply Dr. Hunt trying hard to believe his own eyes.

CHAPTER FIFTEEN

I GAVE a bow and a hiss and tried to ease a very tense situation by laughing lightly.

"Well, what next..." Dr. Hunt gasped.

"Did they tell you I was missing?" I said. "I came back. I came into Laboratory H to report, but there was some kind of 'conference' going on."

"Yes?"

"So I thought I'd wait by your chair and tell you when you came in. I think you should know what they were talking about..."

Dr. Hunt mopped his forehead and stroked his mustache and beard. Then he gathered his faculties together and began to talk, heedless of what I was about to tell him.

"As you know, I've been getting you ready for a special job on the outside," he said. The glint in his eye told me that he considered it important for me to listen closely and indulge in no foolishness. He motioned me to stand to one side. I waited by the wall while he gave Winston a few slaps, trying to bring the man around. Winston came up nodding and blinking, and sat blankly while Dr. Hunt gave me further information and instructions.

"You came back to the lab this evening after being free on the outside for awhile—am I right?" Hunt asked.

"Right," I said.

"Then I trust you'll come back again," he said. "I'm going to depend on it. In fact, I'm going to show you that I have a great deal of faith in your loyalty."

I was a tad suspicious of what he was saying, but I didn't

cast any expressions that might hint as to whether I might or might not be as loyal as he needed me to be. My loyalty certainly depended on his plans for turning me into a museum piece. However, for the moment I felt that the good doctor would postpone that unpleasantness for at least the foreseeable future.

"I'm going to send you on this assignment at once," Dr. Hunt said. "Come this way and I'll show you the map of the primary Masha territory once more."

I looked at Dr. Hunt. The expression on his face was most serious. It appeared there would be no more questions about my absence from the complex. Instead, he was going to press me into service without further ado.

I might have complied without any hesitation, and considered it an honor—if I hadn't caught a sidelong glance from Winston, who was sitting there, watching me with a cold eye. The fellow was still badly shaken, I knew. He kept rubbing his sides where my scales had clutched him. But I knew the real core of his anxiety was because he knew I had overheard his conversations prior to Hunt's entry into the lab.

"This way," Dr. Hunt repeated. It was so odd, seeing someone motion to me with three or four arms.

I stamped about, folded my lower legs under me, and rose high on my forelegs, craning my neck and head upward as if I meant to be heard. I caught a glimpse of myself reflected in some of the glass utensils, and my very pose helped to inspire me for what I needed to say.

"It's time, Dr. Hunt, that you and I cleared the air between us," I said.

The doctor's beard gave an impatient twitch, but he stopped cold and stood listening.

"I came here from Earth for a purpose," I said. "I came in the guise of a pilot for businessman, Ernest Macklin, who is planning a commercial enterprise from this planet. But my real reason for coming was to get *you.*"

Dr. Hunt placed his hands on his hips. "Why should you want to get *me?*"

"Because you're too useful a scientist to desert the Earth. I was hired to come here and find a way of bringing you back. Your own planet and your own solar system need you immensely."

"I'm doing very well here, thank you," said Hunt. I saw him cast a quick look at Winston before he added, "After all, I'm running the best research laboratory you ever saw. You haven't convinced me that there's anything more advanced on Earth."

"Granted," I said. "But maybe I can convince you that *you aren't running this place.* You should have heard the conversation that took place in here just a short while ago."

"What conversation are you talking about?"

"The conversation I heard between Dr. Winston and a deep-voiced fellow who left the lab just moments before you entered." I bent over, directly into Dr. Hunt's face. "Among other things, they were discussing the way they've been duping you—even controlling your thoughts."

MY WORDS struck hard. Hunt whirled around and looked in Winston's direction.

"They're planning to turn me into a laboratory skeleton," I continued, "and they've somehow forced that plan into your mind—don't ask me how. I only know what I heard. You were all ready to go through with it, too. You've even set up a pedestal for my bones to rest on in the museum. But your own good scientific judgment got the better of you and made you wait. You know that I'm more valuable alive than dead."

The doctor was moving toward me slowly, with a light of curiosity in his face. *"Who* did you say is duping me?" he

SECRET OF THE SERPENT

asked slowly.

"Dr. Winston and some other person"

"What other person?"

"I didn't get a good look at him, but he had a voice like a deep cistern."

Winston sprang to his feet. "Dr. Hunt, please. Don't believe a word of this. This snake fellow is just trying to divert your attention away from his own inexcusable actions."

"Is he?" Dr. Hunt scowled deeply.

"I'll tell you both what I overheard while I was hiding in that chair. The deep-voiced fellow said it wouldn't be good for the two of them to be found here together."

"Very interesting," said the doctor.

"And he tempted Winston to take over your place as the head of this complex."

"Indeed."

"Stop it!" Winston cried. "I'm Dr. Hunt's friend and advisor. My loyalty is unquestioned."

"It has long been rumored, Dr. Hunt," I went on, gesturing with my long arm, "that you were brought to this planet not necessarily of your own free will. Do you admit that much?"

Hunt was too distracted to answer my question. He stood there staring, searching Winston's eyes for the truth.

Winston stepped toward him, both hands extended. "You know I've been loyal to you, Dr. Hunt," he said. "I don't know what to say. This entire story is preposterous. You *know* I'm your friend. Please don't to listen this…this…"

"He's a snake by an accident of fate," Hunt cut in. "But if he's lying, I'll see that he's…." He turned to me. "…boiled in oil. What did this deep-voiced fellow looked like?"

"I didn't see him," I said. "I only saw the shadow of what looked like a big skull."

"How big was he?"

"I don't know. It was dark, and after I hid in the chair I couldn't turn to see, even after the lights went on. But I'd know his voice in a moment."

"Which way did he go?"

"Out that door. After you rung for the power chair, he told Winston it was time for him to leave."

Winston began to laugh. "This is ridiculous." He mocked my words thoroughly.

There wasn't much more I could say or do at this point. I had played my hand and I was losing. It wasn't easy for Dr. Hunt to suddenly place a great deal of trust in a newcomer like me. I had already pulled my share of snaky tricks earlier in the evening, and this might simply be another. I had no pocket to pull out a fistful of credentials to prove that a group of Earth scientists had sent me here to bring him back. I only had scales and a pair of deceitful looking eyes and a monstrous form that made men shudder to look at me.

"If you'll pardon me," said Winston, "I think I'll go take a bath. This whole incident has left me feeling a little unclean."

That was all he needed to say. *I was just an unclean snake.* Any warning truths I might offer were just *so much hissing.*

"I'll give you some pointers on the new experiment a little later, Dr. Winston. I'll talk to you in the morning." Dr. Hunt spoke with his usual professional manner—and that was enough to convince me that I hadn't dented the bond that existed between the two. Dr. Hunt turned to me. "As for you my friend, you can either go out on the assignment we discussed or return quietly to your cage. Which will it be?"

CHAPTER SIXTEEN

I MOVED along at a slow, thoughtful crawling pace through the remainder of the night, watching the last of the six moons slide silently through the skies.

The air was fresh and fragrant, and I was glad to be away from the odors of the mountain fortress. A whiff of blossom scents caused me to turn my course toward the long jagged black line, far down the valley, which I knew to be the crevasse.

That crevasse, with its river about a mile below the upper surface, had offered me plenty of pain since I had first fallen into this weird world. But it was not like the pain that I suffered now—the pain of not being trusted. Strange to say, I felt a nostalgic attraction for the crevasse again, and part of me wished that I might return to its rocky walls and bathe again in its warm waters.

What a mood!

I was nursing my jumbled emotions. I was discouraged because Dr. Hunt hadn't toppled at my first invitation to abandon his set-up on Space Island and come back to the Earth with me.

I was discouraged and disillusioned because Dr. Winston had so quickly collapsed from my view of him as a fine research doctor, to a sinister, conniving villain.

Was he that, though? Somehow I continued to cling to a sliver of hope that he wasn't. If the person with the deep-cistern voice had managed to put some kind of malicious bug inside Dr. Hunt's brain, perhaps he had done the same thing to Dr. Winston. Perhaps he was duping *both* of them.

I looked back to the road that led to the mountain fortress. I regretted coming away before finding out more about the strange being with the deep-cistern voice. Could it have been a transformed creature of some sort with a heavy human skull—a deep throat—soft swishy feet?

I grew weary. To the side of the road I found a grassy spot to rest on. As I lay on the soft grass, I closed my eyes and sifted through all the recent events in my half-sleeping mind. I soon found my thoughts returning to the missing

Ernest Macklin. I wondered about his whereabouts. Would Flora ever see him again? How long ago it all now seemed. I thought back to our original flight to Space Island...

I RECALLED that we had been flying through space for only a short period of time when Flora first discovered that Macklin had deceived her.

"Where is my female companion?" Flora had asked.

"I told you there'd be a female companion to travel with you," Macklin had answered matter-of-factly, "and I've kept that promise. Now please stop your silly worrying."

It was Flora Hessel's first trip away from Earth, and although I usually stayed pretty busy inside the control room, it was sometimes hard not to accidentally eavesdrop on the conversations of others within the next room. I knew she was uneasy about her situation. I dreaded to think that she might be in an anxious state all the way to Space Island.

"But who is she?" Flora then asked. She was being reasonable and patient.

Ernest Macklin lit a cigar and began to pace uneasily. I saw that his first mate, Pete Hogan, was getting nervous, watching to see what Macklin meant to do. *I* knew, and Hogan must have known, that there wasn't any other lady on board the ship.

"Your companion's name is Terry," said Macklin. "Ma Terry. She's in the second stateroom having a nap. No use waking her. She's a safe enough companion for anyone. She likes people and she has a soft heart, just like you, Miss Hessel. The two of you ought to get along just fine."

I SAW Pete Hogan gulp. He didn't say a word. Whenever Ernest Macklin made a statement, it stood; Hogan was not one to cross him up.

Macklin came toward the control room, his wide

shoulders filling the doorway for a moment. He saw that I was busy, and blowing a puff of smoke in my direction, he closed the door on me so I wouldn't hear anything further.

But I was curious, so I set the controls and cracked opened the visor that gave me a view of the next room.

Flora Hessel was getting angry and suspicious. When Macklin tried to divert her from her questions by putting an arm around her, she became angry. She wasn't in the mood for his patronizing affections. All she wanted was to see Ma Terry.

I opened the door a crack to hear the conversation.

"Pete, get Ma Terry," Macklin said to Hogan, chomping angrily on his cigar.

"If you say so."

"I said so, didn't I? Get her."

"Miss Hessel may be kind of disappointed," Hogan said dubiously.

"Be quiet and do as I say…"

Hogan shrugged. I could see him go through another door and down a short hall to the second stateroom. He opened the door and whistled. "Come, Terry."

Out came a little black and white terrier dog.

"She's a Mamma Terrier," Macklin said out of curled lips. "We call her Ma Terry for short. That's your female companion, Miss Hessel. I always keep my promises. She's gentle and softhearted, just like you. Like I said, the two of you ought to get along just fine."

Flora walked up to Macklin, anger written all over her face.

"You lied to me," she said, a seething undertone in her voice.

"Did I?" Macklin answered back. He then flashed an almost imperceptible smile. "I didn't think you'd really mind." He raised his hand again and placed it on her shoulder.

Flora then slapped him in the face.

Macklin's face then went completely red. He raised a fist as though to strike her. Hogan gestured for him to stop, and gulped a scared, "Don't do it—*don't!*"

But I was the guy who dashed in and put the strong-arm on his own boss in time to keep Flora from getting her teeth knocked out. One solid uppercut to his jaw did the trick. He collapsed into a corner for several minutes. Hogan tried to bring him to.

Flora kept to her room most of the time after that, though she occasionally came into the main room when several of us were gathered there—for lunch, or a game of cards, or a round of sky-study. Macklin, who initially threatened to throw me into the brig, decided against it when Flora threatened to file various charges against him when we reached Space Island. Macklin had miscalculated the situation completely. He had obviously thought Flora would fall into his arms, not because he was so very handsome, but because he was her employer and was able to talk in big terms about his nebulous commercial ventures, which were ready for launch when we reached Space Island.

After that Macklin kept his temper under control for the most part. However, it did burst out again during one incident midway through the flight. Flora had made friends with Ma Terry and had gotten in the habit of feeding the dog right after the crew's lunchtime. She often talked to it in an affectionate manner, just as she might have talked to a young child. Macklin had watched with growing jealousy. Shortly before lunch one day, the dog got under his feet by mistake. He gave it a quick kick. It whimpered, so he kicked it again. Flora asked him to stop and that was all he needed. In a fit of anger, Ernest Macklin kicked Ma Terry to death. The rest of the crew was horrified.

After the dog was disposed of, Macklin walked back and forth throughout the ship, eyeing any of us who happened to be talking, as if daring us to criticize his action. It was a horrible situation for everyone on board.

It was a pretty unhappy trip, after that. Macklin and I went toe to toe a couple of times, but were separated before any blows were thrown. And so it had been, as we approached Space Island, that he and I were keeping an eye on each other like two suspicious hawks.

Then came the day of the landing. I'll never forget it. The ship had slowed down and was descending through the atmosphere. We were just able to see through the clouds to the surface below when an unaccountable explosion struck through the ship. There was an ear-shattering sound and a blinding white light. That was the last thing I remembered until I found myself in the dark water, deep down in the crevasse, many hours later. It was then that I discovered I had become a serpent…

NOW THE new day was dawning. I had fallen asleep hours earlier, curled up on the edge of a thicket whose greenish-blue hues camouflaged me from the eyes of any chance passers-by. The weight of my troubles had made me weary and I thought I would sleep the forenoon away. And I might have, if a spaceship hadn't exploded while zooming down from the sky above.

CHAPTER SEVENTEEN

THE explosive qualities of Space Island were a fact to be reckoned with. Explosions were Space Island's official welcome, it seemed, for everything that dropped down out of the skies.

I had gone through it once myself. Later I had seen it

happen to a dead spaceship that had floated in aimlessly. Now I was seeing it for the third time.

This was a shapely, well-knit ship that was obviously cruising into the atmosphere for a landing. The deadly invisible trap caught it, and suddenly the splinters of wreckage were falling over a range of several miles, drifting down like so many feathers. I discerned a few human bodies among the falling objects. They were alive and kicking. Transformed? It didn't appear so. But soon perhaps!

Two of the falling men wore blue uniforms, and one of these fell within a short distance of my hiding place. I sprang to my feet and went into a high-powered snake gallop, using my swiftest crawling muscles to give myself an extra boost from the belly with every leap.

I stopped within a few dozen yards of the fallen officer. I hid behind some shrubbery and waited.

He had struck easily, not like a man falling to the Earth, but with the airiness of a balloon. He was sufficiently stunned, however, that he crawled off dizzily on his hands and knees. I wanted to help him, but I knew I might scare the poor fellow out of his wits if he saw me. Instead I followed from a fair distance, keeping him in sight.

He was still in human form. But he crawled to a nearby pool of water, and as soon as he began to drink and to bathe his face, *it* happened.

It was an amazing sight to watch.

His clothing began to fall away from him. He was resting on his hands and knees over the water. His neck and head began to take on a beast-like shape. He let out a horrific squeal as his body shortened and his legs contracted into the legs of pigs. Legs, feet, ears, snout!

He had transformed into a wretched, grunting hog!

He looked back at his clothes and gave a snort of disgust. The poor creature seemed to be dazed. With his front feet in the edge of the pool and his snout burrowing senselessly in the mud, he let his eyes fall closed and fell comfortably to sleep. It had all happened within a few minutes of the explosion.

Later I was to learn from Kipper more about the unusual forces behind these incredible events involving exploding spaceships. And what I learned was shocking. The force that caused the spaceships to explode wasn't anything natural to the planet, but a powerful ray of some type that emanated from a horizontal projector imbedded in the mountains somewhere above the scientists' fortress. It and others like it guarded the entire planet from the dangers of falling objects from space, which had been a problem on the planet for centuries. If giant meteors fell through space and into the atmosphere, the invisible rays would break them into pieces and retard their fall to the surface, thus preventing widespread damage from the falling debris. But how the rays were able to retard objects from falling to the surface at full speed was unclear, even to Kipper. This was undoubtedly what had saved the lives of all who had fallen from exploding spaceships, including Flora and myself. But the ray did not cause transformations. Those were produced by certain *natural* elements on the planet itself.

I looked beyond the sleeping pig, remembering there were other fallen men nearby. One of them I spotted less than a mile away. He had come through with no damage whatsoever. He was walking slowly toward the low foothills that lay pink in the morning light. I slipped along cautiously for many yards, then stopped abruptly when I heard him call out. Was he crying for help? I crawled closer until I was able to hear him.

"A message for the Mashas!" he shouted out to the foothills. *"A message for the Mashas!"*

No, he wasn't out of his head. He appeared to know

exactly what he was doing. It seemed obvious that he and the rest of his small party had come with the intention of making contact with the Mashas, so it wasn't surprising when a delegation of a dozen pygmies came running out of the foothills to greet him a few minutes later.

But why? What was going on?

I then spotted another of the fallen spacemen moving along, also near the foothills. He, too, was calling out the same message.

FIVE low, but very large artificial earthen mounds provided the official entrance to the main Masha settlement, an underground city. An arched opening in the center mound was just large enough for these wayfarers from space to enter—bent over at the waist. The twelve Mashas followed them in and I was left to wonder what it was all about.

I can't say why I crawled back to the sleeping pig at the edge of the pool—unless it was because my appetite was rising. But as I approached, I looked back toward the fortress to see that a squadron of planes had roared out of the mountain and was now flying up and down the valley. That was how it had happened before—the scientists had sent out search planes and search parties to pick up the pieces, and also to reconvert any "transformed survivors" into their original human forms. Unless of course they were interesting enough in their design to deserve a place in Dr. Hunt's research labs.

On one of the plane's passes, someone—or rather, *something*—was spotted. I didn't get there in time to see what sort of monstrosity it was. But the plane had already circled down to fly over within a few feet of the surface of a fast-running stream. Out went a package of yellow powders.

Pwooft!

A small explosion of dust and steam followed. Flora Hessel should have been here to see it, I thought. This was exactly the way it had happened to her. When the cloud cleared, the subject walked out in his normal human form—a fine looking human specimen.

A blimp then came over and a basket was dropped for the fellow. He finally got in, under protest. I could only assume that his original destination had also been the camp of the Mashas. All of which meant that this particular party of Earthmen had come with some special purpose for contacting the Mashas. I could only speculate as to why.

Once again I hurried back to the sleepy, grunting beast that I had left at the edge of a pool. He had appeared to be an officer before his transformation, so I knew he wouldn't be forcibly taken away by a search squadron too easily.

But the planes never spotted him. The pygmies found him first. Three of them came upon him, all of them gripping *zeego* guns. I stayed hidden in the dense vegetation.

Several guns flashed in succession. I held back, hardly breathing. Once again I thought Flora Hessel should be here to see what was happening, for she too had been the target of *zeego* fire. Would it work again?

Yes...*he began to change.*

The three pygmies approached cautiously. From a grunting hog into a muttering officer—the transformation was extraordinary.

He had lost a share of his dignity with the loss of his clothes, so the pygmies offered him a wrap to throw around his quivering body. He seemed bewildered and a trifle uncertain of his directions, so he asked for a map that was in his shredded clothing. However, when it was retrieved it was found to be too mutilated to be of any use. The pygmies then conducted him away—toward the five-mound entrance.

I drew a deep breath. My serpent cunning had permitted

me to see a great many things this day, and I was beginning to understand much that I hadn't understood before.

If the planes had found the sleeping hog first, I knew that they would have restored him to normal and taken him back to the fortress, just as they had taken Flora. He would have been pressed him into service as a cook, or an attendant, or a guard, or a laboratory assistant—according to his talent. This was the way the fortress was growing. They might never know that he had come to Space Island with the secret purpose of plotting with the Mashas.

MOREOVER, I was finally beginning to understand the series of conditions and events that appeared to underlie all of the weird physical transformations on the planet. And it gave me new hope—hope that I, too, might find a way back to normalcy.

It was a three-part situation.

The first part was born out of man's ingenuity—the effects of the hidden ray guns that the scientists had planted in the mountains of Space Island.

The second part was nature's own, and it must have been operating for centuries. It appeared that certain waters in the region played biological havoc on the bodies of newcomers who, by drinking them, found themselves physically transformed in the most astonishing way. Could it be that one was somehow transformed by the waters into the type of creature that last drank from them?

The third part was the physical undoing of nature's transformations. This appeared to be something that was accomplished by certain types of physical shock. *Zeego* fire appeared to be one method. Yes. The explosions of the strange yellow powders appeared to be another. Were reconversions possible with other explosions or concussions? There was no way to tell for sure, but it certainly seemed possible.

I was beginning to feel hopeful, for at last I was seeing a way back from my awful predicament. Perhaps even a way to complete my original mission. If I wanted Dr. Hunt to listen to my pleading, I knew I first needed to return to human form. Then I could return to the mountain fortress and implore him to hear me.

It was a hopeful moment for me, but I couldn't be too optimistic. My skin had already proven too hard-crusted for any real effect from *zeego* guns. As for the powders, I had already withstood two explosions and each time had been only partially restored.

For the remainder of the day I lolled around, devising all manner of shock treatments for myself. I imagined throwing myself over the side of a mountain, but the memory of my fall through the crevasse gave me an awful shudder. I could always leap under the wheels of a speeding truck. That, however, might prove more physically damaging than concussive in effect. I wondered if heat might play a factor? Perhaps I could start a large fire and leap into it. Maybe more intense *zeego* fire was needed. I could creep into the ranks of the guards at the fortress and start devouring them so they would spray me with their ray guns. I smirked at the thought of it.

None of these plans appealed to me as being pleasant, and I had visions that any one of them might ultimately prove to be fatal. I wanted to restore myself to normal, but I didn't want to kill myself in the attempt. After all, it was better to live as a serpent than to die as a man.

"It is better to live as a serpent," I said to myself several times, "than to die as a man."

I found myself growing fond of that conclusion. I was a serpent, but at least I had my human memory and most of my normal faculties of reasoning, only slightly permeated by serpent instincts. Perhaps I should leave well enough alone.

"It's not so bad being a serpent," I told myself, "after you get your belly toughened up."

And so, after crawling through a maze of mysteries, I was beginning to find myself.

I approached the mounds quietly.

CHAPTER EIGHTEEN

THE Mashas were inside their mounds, warm and comfortable, no doubt. A light rain was sprinkling down over my forty-foot form, and I shivered with the thought that the waters of Space Island might transform me again and take away my arms and legs.

But no, I had encountered rains before with no ill effects. I was probably safe. My theory of transformation might be scientifically naive, but I felt fairly certain I didn't need to fear the rain.

I soon reached the mounds and tried my best to walk gingerly over them as I approached the entry point to the Masha underground city. The mounds were actually quite vast, not in height, but in width. They were structures of softened earth, so I was not only leaving a twisted path in the moistened dirt, but I was probably causing pieces of Masha roofs to fall in.

Clunk!

I heard the screech of annoyed Masha voices below me. I had probably knocked half a ton of earth down on their supper! I scurried down into the depression between the mounds that led to the entrance of the honeycombed city.

My thoughts went back to the newly fallen visitors from Earth. *Why had these newly arrived Earth people been welcomed here? What strange plans were being made within these mounds?*

Low voices were welling up through one of the open

ventilators of a nearby mound, so I crept up to the crest of its earthen roof. They were Masha voices. A number of wizened little officials were in conference. They were sitting on the earthen floor, their bronzed bodies highlighted by a flickering red fire. I was stunned by what I heard them discussing.

"We lost one of them to the blimp," one was saying. "They'll hold him at the fortress indefinitely unless we invade and rescue him. But Macklin says there isn't time. We attack tomorrow morning."

"But we still rescued the other three. If these three Earthmen are as clever as Macklin claims, we'll have a fighting chance to win this time."

Macklin? Ernest Macklin? Was he somehow mixed up in this intrigue? I was holding my breath for fear I'd gasp too loudly into the ventilator shaft.

They were planning to storm the fortress again—soon. The newly arrived men were probably mercenaries or tactical advisors that were on the Macklin payroll. There was much concern that one of them had been whisked away by the blimp and taken to the scientists' fortress.

"The same thing happened to the woman that Macklin brought with him. What did he call her…a *special* employee? But the men from the fortress got her, too."

"We should have rescued both of them."

"Well, who's to blame? You were the closest to her. You saw for yourself that she'd turned into a two-headed cat creature. All you had to do was give her another blast from your *zeego* gun."

"Stop harping about it. Besides, we'd have gotten her if that serpent creature hadn't appeared out of nowhere."

"So you stopped shooting?"

"He *got* one of us as it was!"

"You might have turned your gun on him."

"But Macklin didn't want him—not alive, I mean. Let the scientists have their fun with him. They've probably dissected him by now."

Their grumblings were suddenly interrupted by a wizened courier who entered from a side door. He brought with him a message from Ernest Macklin.

"What does it say," one of them asked.

"We're having a pre-invasion assembly tonight."

"Pre-invasion?" someone said skeptically. "I'm beginning to have second thoughts about this entire plan. Who is this Ernest Macklin anyway? He speaks in glorious terms about helping us, but why should we put so much trust in him? What does he have to gain by helping us free our enslaved brothers? He says his 'economic ventures' will help us develop a real, working economy for our people. But somehow I just don't buy it. Besides, earlier today I received inside information that Macklin may really be planning something else."

"Something else?"

"Yes. Those new ships he's reconstructed are all set for a space flight. My informant believes he's going to force the whole lot of us to some other planet to start a new colony."

"So what if he does?" another voice added. "After we free the slaves from the fortress it might be good to have a fresh start. I'm sick of this planet. If that's his plan, and the conditions are right, I might actually be in favor of it."

ALTHOUGH MY view was obstructed, I could tell there were at least a dozen pygmy officials in the room. There was considerable dissention over what Macklin might be planning for them. The official plan from Macklin was that spaceships would be used to fly over the fortress and blanket it with bombs. Mashas would not only help run the ships, but other Masha volunteers would be aboard and used for a ground assault to be launched afterward.

But the rumor was spreading that Macklin's real plan would also include transporting the Masha populace to a new colony on a distant planet.

All of that had left me guessing. What was Macklin's commercial angle? He wasn't playing missionary to these downtrodden outcasts for nothing. One could be sure that he had his eye on the dollar sign. But so far, I couldn't see the dollar in it.

In fact, I hadn't even *seen* Ernest Macklin since the day of the explosion. I hadn't even been sure that he had come through alive.

The pygmies' meeting broke up and I spent the next hour moving around from mound to mound, listening through various openings. It was when I reached the farthest mound that I smelled it, coming up through a ventilator shaft...

Cigar smoke.

A moment later I was looking down through the triple-tiled ventilator at Ernest Macklin—in person.

His cigar smoke had led me to what appeared to be his own Masha headquarters. He was pacing, smoking, waiting impatiently. Around him were a number of Earthmen—the three who had arrived earlier in the day and several men from the original flight I had piloted.

"Miss Hessel should be here soon," Macklin said, glancing at his watch. "We need her to help win the assembly over. The whole Masha leadership will trust us if she presents things properly."

"They won't trust us very long," someone said. "Not after we take off."

"I don't give a damn about that," Macklin snorted. "Just so long as we get them aboard the ships. As soon as we're out in space it makes no difference. Before they ever wake up to what's coming, we'll have them unloaded and sold as *slaves."*

Nobody seemed surprised to hear these words. The men were all part of a well-organized scheme. They talked of lining their pockets with slave profits, and Macklin assured them that the interplanetary market where the slaves were to be sold paid off in very lucrative amounts.

The other part of Macklin's conspiracy was the taking over of the scientists' fortress. There was immense commercial value to the scientific work that was done there, and Macklin was giddy at the thought of controlling the valuable research trade that had been growing there for many years. The plan was clear—use the Mashas to oust the scientists, then ship them off into slavery. There was a clear profit at both ends of the plan.

The fortress had been, in a very real sense, a sitting duck for many years. There were no direct ties with any planetary government. It had always been a private enterprise. It was thought that Hunt and Winston currently held some type of controlling interest, but no one knew for sure. Scientists came and went, and there were persistent rumors that a mysterious, unknown party actually controlled the goings-on there and elsewhere on the planet. One thing was certain, though, there was no one to come and rescue the scientists in the event of an attack.

"Once we have control of the fortress, and once the Mashas are gone, we'll have accomplished everything we set out to do," Macklin told his men.

As I listened on, there was a little sentimental talk about Pete Hogan, who had disappeared after falling over a precipice.

"Poor Pete," Macklin said, "he was the best yes-man I ever had."

Hogan had fallen into the depressed stream, just as I had done. The conclusion was that he had changed into a fish.

SECRET OF THE SERPENT

Macklin had sent a group of pygmies to search for him, but they had been attacked by a serpent—me!

"Who was that devilish serpent?" someone asked.

"Probably my pilot, Bob Garrison," Macklin said. "I'll rest easier when I know they've run him through the lab and scoured his bones. He was a troublemaker. Besides, I think he had his own plans. Something about returning Emerson Hunt to Earth."

"There's no chance of that happening," said one of the new arrivals.

"No, not as long as the White Head keeps both of the doctors under his control," Macklin replied.

The *White Head!*

I instantly thought of the shadowy white skull I had glimpsed inside Laboratory H.

Macklin added, "Have no fear about our plan, gentlemen, especially concerning the White Head's involvement. As I have assured you, *he plays both sides of the fence.* I have his full approval of our plans and he'll be cooperating with us completely."

THROUGH the darkness I picked up the sound of other voices. A party was approaching the earthen city from somewhere down the valley. Within a few moments the footsteps were thudding softly through the underground passages and presently they came into Macklin's headquarters. It was a party of pygmies—I recognized Padderman and Jallan whom I had once encountered on the fortress roofs— and they brought with them a woman.

"I told you we'd succeed," one of them gloated.

Macklin complimented them and dismissed them. Then he and his guests viewed the prize that stood before them: beautiful, black-haired, dark-eyed Flora Hessel. Her face was tilted upward in a characteristically proud pose, and I could see fearlessness in her firm lips.

Macklin stepped up and put his hands on her shoulders as if he possessed her.

"Well, well, so you've finally come back to me. My little sweetheart is all dressed for a party, isn't she?"

She was wearing a fragile pink and white dress that must have been a gift from someone at the fortress. She responded to Macklin's approach in the manner of a prisoner rather than a sweetheart.

"Why am I here, Ernest?" she asked firmly.

"Relax," Macklin said. "You're among friends. And please remember that your services are still under contract to me."

Having introduced the other members of his party, he proceeded to go over his plans step by step. But his story was altered dramatically for Flora's benefit. He said not a word about pressing the Mashas into slavery—nothing like that. He was going to take them to a new planet after their assault on the scientists' fortress and allow them to start a new colony. It all sounded very humanitarian.

And all that Flora needed to do was help "get them in the mood" to accept his magnanimous offer.

"This may require a woman's touch," he added.

Flora seemed uneasy about this. She had done humanitarian work on Earth, but there was something not quite on the level with Macklin's plans. She looked away as though deep in thought.

"The four spaceships are completely ready," Macklin continued, beaming with pride over his cleverness. "At dawn…"

I was incensed over what I was hearing, but I was interrupted by a slight tap on my arm. I almost jumped off the mound.

"Move over," came a tiny whisper in my ear. "I want to see, too."

"Kipper!" I whispered loudly.

"In person. Pleased to meet you."

"What are you doing here?"

"I had to keep an eye on our lady friend," he whispered. "How'd I know you'd already be here?"

"Listen," I said. "There's a devilish plan afoot. Do you know about it? Get an earful of this…"

We both listened. Macklin continued to expatiate on his plans, pouring it on thick. I couldn't tell if Flora was being convinced or not.

"You'll speak to them at the assembly," he was saying, "to help reinforce the sincerity of our promises. Your primary goal is to convince them that a fresh start on a new planet is the best thing for them—that this planet no longer has anything to offer them. You must appear honest in everything you say and do—and how can you miss? You can discuss with them the running their own kingdom. Who knows how leaving this planet may affect them physically? It's possible they may even grow into strong men again on another world. *Strong men again*—that's a good point and a good angle. Who knows…someday they may even have a chance to fall in love with a beautiful woman like yourself."

Flora answered with an edged tone of sarcasm, "Shall I promise them *female companions,* like you promised me on the trip out here? How deep is your supply of terriers, Mr. Macklin?"

Macklin gave off a pompous laugh and looked at the other men in the room. "Yes…just a little joke, gentlemen. Don't mind Miss Hessel. She's always been a bit of a jokester."

CHAPTER NINETEEN

I WANTED to hug Flora for what she had said, but under the circumstances all I wanted to do was somehow let her know that she had friends up on the crumbling mud rooftop. The simplest way was to put my nose to the ventilator and breathe deep.

"*Sssss!*"

"What's that?" said one of Macklin's men, looking up abruptly. I knew he couldn't see anything through the blackness above the ventilator. But Macklin went pale for a moment and moved back.

"Was it Mashas?" someone asked. "I hope we haven't been overheard."

"It's not Mashas," said Flora in a tone that comforted me. "It's only a breeze from the river."

"We'd better get on to the assembly," Macklin said abruptly.

Kipper and I went down into the Masha city together. I would have become totally lost without his help. The tunnels were endless. Most of them were unlit. But the Mashas knew their way around from an almost instinctive sense of direction, and Kipper, like the others, had been here for most of two centuries.

He straddled my neck and clung tight, whispering directions in my ear. Part of the time we moved along at a gallop. There were some areas of the tunnels where I couldn't use my legs because the ceilings were quite low, so we squirmed along the earth in traditional serpent fashion.

"All foot tracks lead to the assembly," Kipper would say whenever a lighted room showed us the tracks of those who had gone before.

"It won't be an assembly if they see *me,*" I said. "It'll be a stampede."

Kipper assured me that he would get me into the underground assembly chamber without creating any undue disturbance, and he made his promise good. We crept in by way of a natural rock shelf about ten feet above the level of the main Masha path. There we huddled, within full view of the torchlight's.

Several hundred Mashas were assembled before us, looking across the cavernous chamber toward a cubical baked-mud platform. On it stood Ernest Macklin. It appeared many of the pygmies were being swayed by Macklin's eloquence.

Waving his arms and talking like a politician who is about to save the country with a plethora of empty promises, Macklin brought his speech to a ringing conclusion.

"By the end of tomorrow, Mashas shall again be a proud people. The battle will be over, and you will be in possession of this land that is rightfully yours."

Hundreds of pygmies applauded with shouts.

"No longer will you be outcasts of space—fugitives from the Earth and from Mars. You will be masters of your own destinies. And as for the scientists who have invaded this realm, they will be your servants, and with their own scientific means we will force them to make you fully human again! However, there is something else that may offer an even greater opportunity for your people. Here to tell you about it is a close friend and colleague, Miss Flora Hessel..."

During the burst of applause that followed, Macklin helped Flora to the platform. She looked out over the multitude of torch-lit faces, and somehow I knew she wasn't going to say exactly what Emerson Macklin had wanted her to say.

The Mashas continued applauding as they waited for her to speak. Flora stood there for a few moments, soaking up the cheers and applause. She believed the Mashas were going to be put back on board the spaceships after the battle, to seek out another planet for a new colony.

"I wonder if she's really going to try and sell it to them," I whispered to Kipper.

"Sell what?"

"Leaving here for a new planet."

Kipper smirked a little at this. "Even Macklin doesn't know what's really going to happen," he whispered back to me. "He *thinks* his ships are going to take them off to a new world—to be sold as slaves. But he's going to be fooled. There won't even be an attack on the fortress..."

I looked at Kipper. I had never seen him quite like this. There was an expression on his face that seemed almost sardonic.

"How do you know?" I said. "Aren't his plans set and ready to go?"

"Oh yes...he thinks they are, but he's overlooked one important fact. There's a more powerful trickster in the mix—the *White Head.*"

FLORA WAS starting to speak. It was a breathless audience.

"I have been brought all the way from the Earth to speak to you," she began slowly. "On the Earth I have helped many people who are trying to regain a solid grip on life. Mr. Macklin has told me that you consider yourselves outcasts, and he thinks that you deserve some sort of victory to salve your injuries from two centuries ago."

"Yes! Yes!" Half the crowd jumped to their feet, waving their arms and shouting in a fervent affirmative.

She quieted them, then continued, "And while I believe your enslaved Masha brothers should be freed from the fortress, *I do not entirely agree with Ernest Macklin.*"

A cry of surprise went up from the crowd.

"I think you have your own good world here," Flora went on, "Mr. Macklin wants me to convince you that a new start on a new planet would be best for all of you. But I think it is childish for you to nurse the injuries of so long ago. I think

Mr. Macklin and your own leaders are doing you a disfavor to stir these old resentments—"

A volley of boos thundered throughout the chamber—a chorus that Macklin and his associates joined. Flora had said all she dared. They would mob her if she said more. Macklin moved briskly to the platform staring wrathfully at her.

But just then there was an interruption than no one had expected. Another being entered the chamber from a side door on one of the far walls, and his entrance stunned the crowd into an abrupt silence.

It was the White Head.

My eyes widened at the sight of him. His body seemed to almost glide into the chamber. He was as I remembered him from the events in the lab. A huge white skull on top of a smaller, pygmy-sized body. I might have laughed had it not looked so terrifying.

From neck to toe he was dressed in a skin-tight green silk outfit. Dark green, yet shining. His arms were short blocks of muscle and the feet were like lion's pads. He cast a countenance of immense, fearful power—an unworldly power encompassing both life and death.

As he moved closer to the platform, I could see the awesome magnitude of his enormous white skull. It cast a pale shadow over Flora's face as she climbed down and moved away from the platform. He stopped briefly and surveyed the crowd. The ghastly white skull then held everyone's eye.

The rows of huge white teeth parted, and the deep, hollow translucent eyes seemed to be taking in the face of every person in the crowd.

The White Head paused beside the cubical platform, and when he extended his arm and pressed against the platform's side, it collapsed into a little cloud of dust and was gone.

Then, as if by magic, the surrounding torchlight's grew

dimmer, and the great skull suddenly grew luminescent. It glowed brighter and brighter until there was nothing in the whole room except deep shadows and a glowing white skull.

The skull tilted and turned. Its jaw moved and spoke.

"Come..."

The deep-cistern voice reverberated throughout the entire underground city.

"Come, the ships are ready. The time is now!"

CHAPTER TWENTY

I LOOKED around for Kipper at that moment, but Kipper was gone. It appeared he was right, though. There *was* a more sinister plan afoot than Macklin's scheme of capturing the fortress and converting the Mashas into slaves.

The Mashas began moving. They followed each other in double time, running down through the black tunnels to the concealed plaza where the ships were supposedly ready for take-off.

The White Head stood beside that exit, pointing the way and beckoning to them. Macklin, seemingly confused, led his his entourage, including the pilots of the ships, through the rear door of the chamber. But before half of the assemblage of Mashas had joined the rush and disappeared through the tunnel, the White Head raised a hand to hold back the rest of the assemblage. There would not be room for all at this time, he told the crowd. And with that he disappeared down the exit following the last of the procession.

I wanted nothing more than to go to Flora and give her a safe ride back to the fortress. But would the fortress be safe? Whatever the White Head's scheme might be—it was clear there were going to be some angry Mashas if they discovered there wasn't going to be an attack on the fortress. The poor, suppressed pygmies who were ready for power. Heaven help any man or god or demon of death that might stand in their way.

The torchlight's, which had magically dimmed after the White Head had entered, flared up again as I was creeping down through the remaining crowd. The Mashas started screaming when they saw me. They scattered out of my path, cursing at me and throwing stones. But I reached Flora and the fright faded from her face at the sight of me.

"Thank goodness!" She began running, motioning me to follow. "Hurry. If anyone can do anything, you're the one."

"What's happening?" I cried, chasing after her. We then entered an opening that led to the surface. "Where are we going? Do you even know?"

"Of course I do! It's a different way, but I think we can cut them off!"

She climbed on my back, slapping me first on one side and then the other to direct me as we snake-galloped across the rolling mounds.

"I should have known that Kipper's hunch was right," she shouted in my ears as we whizzed through the night breeze. "Look over there! Do you see where the red lights are? That's where the ships are taking off from. They constructed a massive, deep blast hole. The four ships are sitting in ready at the bottom. There's a surface entryway over there that leads into the complex below." She slapped my side like a horse. "Hurry!"

We were flying across the mounds at a great speed. I prayed they wouldn't cave in under the weight of my thundering feet.

"It doesn't look like the ships have launched yet," I puffed. "Maybe we'll be in time."

"The ships won't fly!" Flora said. "That's what Kipper tried to tell me. He's sure that—"

"What!" I cut in. " Why not? What's his game?"

"It's the White Head's game. Not even Macklin knows about this. Macklin believes that—"

"Wait a minute!" I interrupted again. "When did you last see Kipper?" I demanded.

"When?" Flora shook her head in confusion. "What does that matter?"

A cold suspicion shot through me

"Are you sure Kipper *is* Kipper?" I cried.

I slowed up so fast that Flora had to cling to my neck for dear life. I stopped, turned my head, and faced her in the dark.

"What's the matter with you?" she cried. "Go on. It's the White Head's crimes we want to stop. He's not really putting the Mashas on ships. He's going to lead them into transformation waters—specially concentrated water that will change them for sure. But this time the nature of the transformations will be controlled. Kipper has told me everything. The White Head's going to run them through these waters and then into some ghastly transformation apparatus that will literally disintegrate the flesh off their bones. But they won't actually die. As fast as they change into these new forms, they'll become *living* skeletons."

"What?" I gasped, an incredulous look on my face.

"It's a regular skeleton assembly line, I tell you. *Why don't we go? Are we going to let Kipper fight it alone?*"

"This is craziness!" I shouted. "I think it's Kipper who's double-crossing the whole lot of us! *I think Kipper IS the White Head!*"

"Go! Please go!" That's all Flora could say. I thought she was starting to cry. But I obeyed. With my two serpent eyes fixed on the growing red light I flew into top speed and raced like a ship through space.

CHAPTER TWENTY-ONE

AN ASSEMBLY line of skeletons—I was stunned at the lunacy of it. It sounded like the maddest, blackest moment of the most twisted nightmare imaginable. I shook my head in disbelief, but kept on moving.

We found our way into the lower levels by following the guides of sight, smell, sound, and feeling. Especially sound. I had learned to put an ear to the ground. This way I could catch the direction of the throbbing vibrations that beat faintly through the length of my body. I was convinced the procession of pygmies was finding its way down through subterranean tunnels. Tunnels that also appeared to be alive with electrical vibrations of some sort. Perhaps there were electronically powered machines somewhere ahead.

Flora and I entered a dark tunnel that showed a flare of amber light around an approaching corner. We heard the steady hum of machinery. We crawled, on and on, Flora pressing down close over my shoulders to dodge blemishes in the uneven ceiling. At last the tunnel curved into a high-ceilinged chamber whose orange rock walls grew bright with light that flooded in from an entrance at the far end.

Brighter and brighter the way became, and louder and louder the electronic rumble. We came to a set of open doors and halted, gazing into the chamber beyond. Flora recoiled in horror. Looking out, we both saw it with our own eyes...

A stumbling train of freakish skeletons.

I haven't the heart to describe these strange monstrosities. No two were the same. Very few presented any semblance of balance or symmetry. It was as if they had been shattered into pieces, then reassembled haphazardly.

The line was moving slowly—slowly enough that one

might count ten before the next skeleton emerged from the black circular opening at our left.

"The Mashas—transformed!" Flora gasped in an awed tone. "They're walking into it, one after another, thinking they're on the way to the ships!"

We plunged ahead, up a long flight of stairs, across a balcony, up another stairway, over a catwalk, and down a ramp. It was a frantic scramble. In the back of my mind I was marveling that someone or some thing had organized enough Masha slave labor, in secret, to construct such an elaborate scientific set-up. Whoever was responsible had been able to keep the secret air tight, working scientifically to change the magic waters of the planet into something so potent that even the Mashas' resistant physiology would be vulnerable. And they had diabolically devised a scheme for putting a large share of the population through with one swift stroke.

In my heart I was sick to think that the White Head might be Kipper. I compared the size of the two creatures. Without the massive skull, the White Head's body was about the same size as Kipper's. Was the skull a mechanical contrivance of some sort? Or could it somehow be the real thing? Could Kipper somehow transform into his strange counterpart at will? Who could tell in this land of sudden, bizarre transformations? And what of its mental powers? The White Head certainly seemed to control the mind of Emerson Hunt, possibly even Winston and others. And then there was the dimming of the torchlights in the assembly chamber and the almost hypnotic effect on the Mashas.

I then grimly remembered that Kipper had disappeared shortly before the appearance of the White Head.

I thought back to the night on the rooftops when Kipper had been taken prisoner by Jallon and the others. Had I not intervened would he have simply changed into the White

Head when the hot branding iron hung over his bare skin? Had I really even *saved* him, or was he just toying with his pursuers?

"We'll find the White Head up this way!" Flora said. "One more stairway and through that narrow copper door. *Kipper told me!*"

"Maybe Kipper *showed* you!" I said angrily. My logic told me that if Kipper knew his way through these mysterious chambers then he was undoubtedly part of the sinister goings-on. Or was I simply giving way to wild paranoia?

Flora looked at me, great exasperation on her face. "Why are you angry with me because I want to help Kipper stop these atrocities?" she said. She then swung off my back and stood there on the step, glaring at me. The light reflected off the copper doorway just above us, and it glinted in her eyes dangerously. We were both panting, and all at once I could hardly speak because of my rising anger, but I managed to choke out a few heated words.

"How do you know all about this, Flora? How does *Kipper* know—"

"All right, I'll *tell* you," she nearly shouted. *"Kipper is the grandson of the White Head."*

"What!"

"Yes, Bob. It's true. He told me everything. They were shipped from Mars together a hundred and fifty years ago. The White Head was the only one of the Mashas who was ever transformed by the waters. Kipper said his grandfather was more sensitive, more delicate, and less changed by the conditions on Mars. He was a scientist, and he discovered that it was the Space Island waters—saturated with the strange qualities from certain blossoms—that caused all sorts of physical miracles. So he went to work...and he became the real power here on Space Island...feared and respected, almost like a god, yet always in the background. His transformation gave him almost magical powers of mental and physical control…"

"You're sure," I said, "that this is not Kipper you're talking about?"

"Yes, I'm sure. Kipper told me all about it. He needed someone to confide in, someone from outside the Masha world. What do you think we talked about on our 'dates?' Yes…I'm the one he came to. And all these years Kipper has kept watch, not knowing exactly what his grandfather was planning until just recently. He was afraid to tell, worrying because he didn't dare—"

"But why?" I interrupted. "What could possibly be the White Head's motive? This is absolute madness!"

"Yes…yes it is. And he *is* mad—utterly mad. Kipper has seen this coming for a long, long time. The White Head resented not only the scientists at the fortress, but even more so—his *own* people. He held a simmering, growing resentment over the decades because he was the only one of his kind changed by the waters of Space Island. And think about it…he truly is a horrifying freak of nature. His original transformation left him greatly changed to begin with, and now his senses of logic and science and morality have all been replaced with unchecked hatred and total madness. His horrendous plan is to change his own people into something even worse than he is, not just sardonic skulls with human bodies, but a complete reduction to the basic foundation of a person's physical being—the human skeleton. Don't try to make sense of it, Bob. There is no logic to madness."

We pushed through the narrow copper door.

The thick, sickening perfumes of blossoms filled my serpent nostrils and for an instant I staggered backwards.

The waters were rushing through a large, open conduit. Dark green waters. Deeper in color than the waters of the depressed stream I had originally fallen into. Thickened waters that carried a heightened power of transformation.

One after another, the pygmies were dropping down from an open shaft above the conduit. They fell, kicking and screaming. The conduit was deep, and before they could swim to the edge they were washed along and into a large funnel that emptied them into the transformation apparatus Flora had spoken of.

"Can you make the leap?" Flora cried to me. She pointed to a platform on the other side of the conduit. A desperate struggle was in progress there...

Kipper and the White Head were locked in a fight to the death.

Kipper had a steel bar in his hand. He was trying to slam the White Head over the crown of his skull. One hard blow struck, but seemingly with no effect. The White Head gave an ugly laugh through his immense white teeth. He then slammed his hand into the side of Kipper's head. Stunned, Kipper fell to his knees.

It was a twenty-foot leap over the water and the screaming Mashas who flowed beneath. I caught the opposite side of the conduit with my good hands and whipped my tail against the green waters. Then I came up, fast and strong, and ran toward the two struggling fighters; but before I could reach them, the White Head knocked Kipper off into the water with one hard fling of his hand.

I sprang to the edge of the conduit and reached a hand toward the little fellow as he floundered, *but my arm somehow wouldn't straighten.* I missed him! I caught a glimpse of his grim face as he floated toward the funnel that spilled into the transformation apparatus below. Then I saw Flora lean in at the last possible second and grab him.

"Thank heavens!" I exclaimed. Then I head a low growl from a deep-cistern voice.

The White Head was coming after me.

"The switches!" Flora cried from across the way. She pointed to a nearby wall.

As the White Head closed in on me, I felt one muscle after another becoming paralyzed throughout the left side of my body. Some sort of mind control was being used on me! But I managed to whip my long tail at the wall and strike a row of several switches—striking them *off!*

Almost instantaneously the pygmies ceased to fall from overhead. I had evidently shut down the entry mechanism above. I could only hope that the unsuspecting Mashas in next level up would soon discover they were not walking into an entry shaft to a spaceship, but into a macabre booby trap.

The waters also stopped moving, which I knew would stop the flow of bodies into the transformation chamber below.

The White Head shrieked in anger. Then he attacked me again with his mind. I could feel further paralysis spreading into my body, but I managed to strike him with a good right uppercut to the throat.

His mighty skull pinched down on my hand just as I struck. For an instant we hovered on the edge of the conduit as we both fought for balance. But the weight of my paralyzed side threw us over. We fell together, kicking and striking and biting—and then we plunged into the blossom-scented waters.

CHAPTER TWENTY-TWO

I was still in the water, but I seemed to have blacked out momentarily. I was gasping for air as I grabbed the edge of the conduit. As I raised myself partway up, I saw Kipper, dripping wet, moving across the floor. But he wasn't coming toward me; he was running *from* me. *He was rushing toward another forty-foot green and purple serpent!*

I yelled at him. "Kipper!"

It was obvious he was mistaking this other serpent for me.

"Kipper! Back this way!" I yelled. "It's me, Bob Garrison—over here!"

He turned and looked at me in utter confusion. But how could anyone have understood? I hadn't realized myself what ghoulish transformation had just taken place.

But as I had intoned the words, *"Bob Garrison"* and had heard the deep rumble of my voice echo out into the chamber, I knew something was horribly wrong. I looked at my hands…

They were now completely human!

Then I gingerly reached up and felt it, and recoiled in horror at the touch of it—*the huge skull I now possessed.*

In the strange waters of Space Island there had been an astonishing cross-transformation…

And I now possessed the body of the White Head.

I reeled at the thought of it. Kipper gave a gasp of complete surprise.

"Bob! Is it you? How is it possible…?"

And there, lashing its ugly tail about, was the controlling power of these weird underground death chambers—the power that *had* been known as the White Head—now in the guise of a four-legged serpent! One could only guess at the unfathomable scientific explanation for it.

Kipper realized what had happened—but just too late.

The big jaws of the serpent closed over his head and snapped the life out of his body in one hard stroke!

I will never forget Flora Hessel's scream. I turned and saw her standing there, the sound of her scream still echoing off the chamber walls. How could she ever believe that it wasn't me who had taken the life of her friend at that horrible moment?

The serpent then plunged back into the water and came

straight for me. I scrambled up over the edge of the conduit. It was in the next instant that I realized the full power that the White Head had possessed—that *I* now possessed. With a vengeful rage in my mind I thought of the row of switches on the nearby wall. Then, as if by magic, all of the machinery came to life again. As the serpent plunged screaming into the flesh-removing apparatus below, I remembered that a pedestal had already been prepared for him.

* * * *

IT WASN'T as difficult as you might think. The greatest advantages were mine, I soon discovered, because I had become the White Head, and there was no one, not even a learned doctor, who did not fully respect my slightest whim. If anything, I was going to have to be very careful not to overplay my power and arouse suspicion.

A word from me to Macklin convinced him that the flights into space would have to be postponed until the Mashas had a better chance to work out plans of their own. I was inclined to agree with Flora that they had a good world of their own right here, where their lives might well go on forever—pleasantly and harmlessly. However, if some of them wished to venture forth to another planet and start a new colony after due consideration, I would see to it that Macklin and his men made good their promises.

My attendants at the fortress found comfortable rooms with bars on the doors and windows for Macklin and his officers, pending the Mashas' decisions. The bars on the door made it possible for persons who felt sociable to stop and say hello to Ernest Macklin now and then, and to bring him a cigar, if they wished. And some of his visitors learned in time to ask if he would like a female companion, and couldn't they bring him a little terrier dog for company?

The numerous Mashas who went through the skeleton transformation process were returned to normal within a few days of their horrible experience. All it took was a little bit of *zeego* fire and a few yellow powder charges.

The original White Head, who was transformed into a living serpent skeleton, was given to Dr. Hunt for research. He was kept in the same cage I had been imprisoned in. But his new skeletal body didn't take too well to the recent transformation, and he was found dead in his cage one morning a few days after his arrival at Laboratory H. He is now one of the prized exhibits of the Museum of Skeletons.

It initially took me several hours of the most earnest discussion to convince my one confidante, Flora, that I was not the White Head, but was still—at heart—a very friendly serpent. I could even remember the time when I had once been Bob Garrison.

"You do seem to be Bob Garrison," she finally said one day as we lunched together on one of the fortress porches. "And you certainly aren't acting like the original White Head."

I tried to smile through my enormous teeth.

"Trust me, Flora, I *am* Bob Garrison—and I remember every moment of our spaceship journey together. Believe me, I fell in love with you on that trip. And one of these days—"

"One of these days, *what?*"

"After I've resolved a few of the problems that only the White Head's power can solve, I'm going to re-submerge myself in the green waters and—hopefully—come back to normal. I'll shoot myself with a *zeego* gun if I have to. So don't go way."

"Problems to solve? You're the mastermind now, aren't you?"

"I'm taking my time," I said. "You see, there was a rather

serious split between Dr. Hunt and Dr. Winston, and now that I've come into this inexplicable power, I can understand how the White Head forced his will over both men. But I can't just go to them and say, 'Dr. Hunt, please understand that Dr. Winston here is really your loyal friend.' "

"Why not?"

"It just won't be as simple at that. But give me some time. They'll both work it out. I know they will..."

A short while later we looked down over the edge of the porch to a plaza below, and there we saw Hunt and Winston engaged in a conversation. Dr. Hunt was speaking, and we caught a fragment of what he was saying.

"I think I understand what you have on your mind, Dr. Winston, but it will do us good to talk it over. I've been thinking I'd like to go back to Earth sometime soon, now that everything seems to be smoothing out. But first I hope that you and I can reorganize our program here...and I mean, reorganize it from the ground up."

I turned to Flora and nodded my huge skull. I felt reasonably sure the two scientists' relationship was on the mend. There would soon be a constructive scientific program rising out of the discarded skeletons of the old.

"It's going to be an interesting world around here as time goes on," I said. "A little less weird, perhaps. And a little less human with poor Kipper gone."

"Much less human without Kipper," Flora said quietly.

"And it will be pretty terrible after you go back to Earth, Flora. Will you be leaving here and going back one of these days?"

Flora smiled. "I've been in love with Bob Garrison for a long time...I think I'll stick around and see what happens."

THE END

THE "SCUM" OF THE SPACEWAYS

That's what the interplanetary police called them. The captain and crew of "the Ghost" were seasoned veterans of outer space, but not with the best of reputations. They were largely outlaws, rebels, and fugitives, coming from all corners of the solar system—creatures of bizarre sizes and shapes. Many of them were horrifying in their appearance, but all were drawn together in a brotherhood of booty. Loyal to their hard-jawed Earthling captain, Wolf Stone.

However, when the Lundars threatened the peace of the system, skilled fighters were needed and the crew of the Ghost stood as one blood with the Crusaders.

CAST OF CHARACTERS

WOLF STONE
From Revolutionary to Raider Chief, his unflinching defiance brought him and his crew across the void.

IVAR
The Ghost's first mate, a Cyclops from Jupiter. He was a dangerous man in any fight.

MEERSA
She was the lovely, young Princess of the Daus. Could she trust the pirates to help save her planet?

ORCUTT
He was the protector of the Princess, but his feelings for her went well beyond loyalty.

RSK
A twelve foot ogre and leader of the Lundars. His primary objective: to turn the Dau race into slaves.

ZNZ
Second in command to Rsk. His mad ambition for galaxy rule went far beyond any loyalty to his leader.

CRUSADE ACROSS THE VOID

By
DWIGHT V. SWAIN

ARMCHAIR FICTION
PO Box 4369, Medford, Oregon   97501-0168

*For more information about Armchair Books and products, visit our
website at…*
www.armchairfiction.com

Or email us at…

armchairfiction@yahoo.com

CHAPTER ONE
Dregs of the Void

THEY dragged the *Ghost's* ruffian crew straight from the hospital laboratories to Tela's great Tribunal Hall.

A strange, wild lot, these raiders—Lizard men of Mars, scaly-skinned, basilisk-eyed, lightning fast; killers as ruthless as cobras, and dreaded from Pluto to Mercury. Shambling, eight-armed Venusians—mechanical geniuses all, deft-fingered and with warm, intelligent eyes. Hard-jawed Earthmen, eternal adventurers of the universe. Saturnians: hairy, chinless, ape-like creatures; two-headed; dull of mind but mightily muscled.

"Scum of the spaceways," the Interplanetary Police called them. "Dregs of the void."

But all fighting men. Roving the vastnesses of a whole solar system as recklessly as Earth's buccaneers prowled the Spanish Main a thousand years before them. From a dozen planets they came—outlaws, rebels, fugitives, drawn together in a brotherhood of booty by one man's will.

That man stood with them, now.

Lean he was, and tall. Brown as the sands of Mercury's sun-scorched wastes. An atavar, crowned with a shock of coal-black hair that marked his blood kinship to some long-dead Comanche chieftain.

Heedless of the *doloid* gyves that shackled him hand and foot, he elbowed his way to the forefront of his captive band.

Earth's Vikings had willed him eyes as cold and pale and blue as the ice of their homeland's glaciers. Now, defiant and unflinching, he met the baleful, red-eyed glare of the Lundars' giant *gar*.

"You *chitzas!*" thundered the chalky Goliath on the Tribunal's throne. "Who are you? Whence come you? What can you say for yourselves?"

The freebooters' lean leader glanced up unconcernedly at the *vocodor-translating* device that gave all men a universe of discourse. He surveyed the great, chill hall, with its gleaming metal walls and its echoing fastnesses. He saw the grim, silent guards, every man twelve pallid feet of rigid discipline. Noted the heavy, unfamiliar pistols that hung low on their hips.

At last he brought his attention back, again to stare, unawed, at the weird, hairless faces of the enthroned Lundar ruler and the aides who flanked him.

The gar hunched forward menacingly, eyes like pools of blood standing out in sharp contrast to the fish-belly white of his skin.

"Well?" he roared. "Answer, you *starbo!*"

The space-rover's thin lips twisted in a contemptuous sneer. When he spoke, his tone was as arrogant as the gar's.

"Who asks us?" he challenged. "Who calls Wolf Stone and his men to account for themselves?" And then, with special, deadly emphasis: "Who *dares* to do it?"

THE twelve-foot ogre on the throne sprang erect.

"I'll have you flayed alive!" he raged, "You'll pray for death—"

"—in the pits of Ra..." finished the Lundar closest beside him. "Indeed they will, Rsk!"

The gar spun on his aide.

"Who asked you, Znz?" he snarled. "You're not yet gar. When I need your advice, I'll ask it."

The Lundar called Znz shrank back into a silence that crawled with fury.

Rsk, the gar, again faced the prisoners.

"You'll learn," he said. "When first we Lundars took Tela, there were many like you here. But now they keep quiet enough—"

"No doubt," Wolf Stone retorted. "But remember, Erk—or whatever your name is—you may find us different. Others have—"

"I'll make you crawl." the Lundar monarch fumed. "My men shall torture you until you beg for death!"

The buccaneer leader's eyes were like blue diamonds.

"We came in peace," he said tightly. "We came a thousand light years across the void from another solar system, our lives suspended in frozen sleep. We hoped, here, to find a welcome.

"But instead, your space ships intercepted ours before the time we were scheduled to waken. Because we were asleep, you didn't have any trouble capturing us. You brought us here. Revived us as prisoners—"

"I thought you'd change your tune," the gar snarled. "Now that you understand I mean what I say, you're crawling already, you *chitza!*"

"No. Not crawling." Wolf Stone shook his head. A mirthless smile played on his thin lips. "No, Rsk. Just giving warning. That's all.

"You say you'll break us. Well, maybe you will. But you'd be wiser to kill us now."

The pirate's smile broadened to a wolfish grin.

"Because, if you don't kill us, you chalk-faced zombie, we'll certainly kill you!" he cried. "If you miss even one of us, may whatever gods you pray to have mercy on your soul—"

"Silence, you fool!"

"Kill us now, or we'll kill you later, Rsk." the lean marauder taunted on, heedless of the giant's wrath. "We'll hunt you down like a rabid *zaroff!* We'll cut you to pieces and leave you to welter in whatever rotten bug-juice it is that fills your veins—"

"Silence!"

The Earthman laughed in the screaming gar's face.

"It's a promise, Rsk…" he shouted. "Wolf Stone's promise! Kill us now, you dog, or we'll see you in hell—"

The Lundar was shaking as with ague. "Take them away!" he shrieked. "Take them away! They'll die by inches—"

BUT all the gar's wild fury could not touch the free-booter chief. He was still mocking the ogrish monarch as the guards dragged him and his band from the hall.

"A short life and a merry one, men!" he cried as they were shoved aboard a subway train far below Tela's surface. "That dough-faced Nero called us in to read us our death warrants. But we gave him his own, instead."

"You think it was smart, though, chief?"

It was the *Ghost's* first mate, Ivar, the band's lone member from Jupiter. He stood a good eight inches taller than his commander's six feet, and outweighed him by a hundred pounds—all of it bone and muscle. He was typical of his race: a hideous, hairless Cyclops, surveying the world through a single, staring eye in the center of his forehead. Four mighty arms made him a dangerous man in any fight, while his bullet head concealed a surprising amount of good sense. And, above all, he worshipped Wolf Stone.

"Smart?" said Wolf. "What do you mean?"

"To roil up this guy, Rsk, so, chief. Like as not he'll give us the ax right now."

The buccaneer leader nodded. "That's right, Ivar. He probably will." The blue eyes flashed. "But no man rides rough-shod over Wolf Stone or Wolf Stone's men, Ivar. Not in this solar system or any other. Die we may, but we'll do it with our heads up, not whining."

"Maybe you're right," the big mate muttered dubiously.

"What else could I do? He was looking for trouble. He was treating us like dogs. No matter what I'd have said, he'd have condemned us. So I decided we might as well shock him a little."

"Shock him!" snorted Ivar. "I'll say you shocked him. I'll bet my pearl-handled ray gun against a bolt of lightning the guy ain't had such a kick in the teeth since the Milky Way went sour." A pause. "Though I got no urge to let these twelve-foot pixies waltz me around if I can help it. Not with Execution Dock for a Maypole."

A broad grin of sheer amusement split Wolf's brown face. Ivar's language was better than any *televo* comic going. Then he sobered.

"We're not dead yet, Ivar," he reminded grimly. "It's one thing to catch us; another to hang on long enough to kill us. The Interplanetary Police can refresh your memory on that, in case you've forgotten."

It was the big mate's turn to grin.

"Yeah," he agreed. "Our outfit don't kill easy. I been condemned so many times now, myself, that I cast a shadow like a gallows. But I guess I wasn't never good enough to die young."

The train jarred to a stop and the guards herded the outlaws into a bleak station, then down a long corridor. At its end was a massive metal door.

"I don't need no X-ray eyes to know there's a jail on the other side of that slab," Ivar grunted.

His chief favored him with a cold grin. " 'Stone walls do not a prison make, nor iron bars a cage,' " he quoted mockingly. "At least, not for Wolf Stone. Remember, Ivar, if one man can build a jail, another can break it!"

THE mate's prediction proved correct. In a matter of minutes the *Ghost's* entire crew was being rigorously searched, put through a routine of registration, and hurried into a huge bullpen cell.

The enclosure already had several occupants. Obviously of a different race than the Lundars, they looked much like Earthmen, and were about the same size, although their skins had the same greyish pallor, as did their giant rulers. All were dressed in rags, and many were gaunt from hunger. Though intelligent in appearance, there was a broken, despondent air about them. They stared up at the space raiders with somber eyes.

"What a bunch of whipped dogs." growled Ivar. "You'd think they were on their way to their own funerals."

Wolf Stone nodded. "Right. And maybe that's it. Maybe all of us are scheduled for our last trip out." He surveyed the dull doloid walls of their prison. Strode across to test the set of the bars cutting them off from the corridor; they were discouragingly solid.

"No windows," commented Ivar sourly, "so we can't make a break that way, like we did on Neptune."

"It's not the getting out that worries me," Wolf said. "It's what we'd do afterward. None of us has even seen the surface of this planet. We wouldn't know which way to go. Like, as not, we'd run right into a bunch of these Lundars who seem to run things around here. And that would be the last of us."

"Yeah. They'd burn us up like magnesium targets."

"What we need," Wolf went on, "is a guide—"

"You want guides, did you say?"

The two buccaneer leaders whirled.

Close beside them stood one of the original occupants of the bullpen. He was a stocky, well-knit young man with a handsome face. And despite the rags, in which he was clad, there was, somehow, a commanding air about him. He lacked the dejection of his fellows. A spark of spirit still burned in his eyes.

"What—?"

"I have a pocket vocodor," the young man explained, pulling aside the remains of his shirt to reveal the instrument's disc. "It was granted me when a few Bans were held here, so that I could act as translator—"

"Bans?"

"Primitives from Suorz. They were taken off to Ra nearly a month ago, just as we shall be tomorrow—"

"Wait." Wolf silenced the other. "Let's get things straight. Just what's going on?"

The young man looked perplexed. "I do not understand. Where are you from, that you do not know the doings of the Lundars?"

THE space pirate's blue eyes searched the young man's brown ones. For a long moment he scrutinized him, weighing all he saw. Then:

"All right. I'll tell you. We're all in jail together, so I can't see that it'll do any harm.

"I'm Wolf Stone. The last of the space raiders—"

"Space raiders?"

"Pirates. Brigands. Outlaws. We held up space freighters for a living. Raided some of the biggest cities in the solar system. A few times we even knocked off whole asteroids."

"Oh. I see." The young man nodded.

"But finally," Wolf went on, "the Interplanetary Police got us holed up on a planetoid near Pluto. They hemmed us in 'til I saw we didn't have a chance in a trillion to get through their lines—"

"This name—" the other broke in, "it is not familiar. Where is this Pluto?"

Ivar snorted in disgust. "Give Wolf a chance to tell you, dope. It's in another solar system. Pluto's the planet farthest out—three-and-a-half billion miles from the sun."

"Yes," the commander continued. "You see, I figured we were just as well as dead. Then our scientist—he's a Uranian—got an idea. He said we should leave the solar system—go out across the void instead of back toward the sun. Then, by setting our unipilots on a charted course for another solar system—"

"But you would die!" expostulated the young man. "No one could live all the hundreds of light years necessary to cross the void from one system to another. It is impossible—"

"But we did it. The Interplanetary Police didn't think that even Wolf Stone would be damned fool enough to leave the system, so they'd only put a skimpy patrol out beyond Pluto. We slipped through like a mosquito through a fishnet.

"Then our scientist put us all in frozen sleep, timed to wake up at the moment when, according to his figures, we'd be in the middle of this universe. Only the Lundars captured the *Ghost*—that's our ship—before we came out of the fog. They revived us in a hospital and took us to a tough customer named Rsk. He sent us here. And that's all we know." A moment's pause. "Now you take it up from there."

The other shook his head as in a daze. "It seems incredible..." he said half-aloud.

Ivar cut him short. "We're here, ain't we?" he grunted. "So quit slobbering about it and angle the set-up for us."

"Yes. Of course." Their new friend smiled. Then: "This planet is called Tela. It is one of the four important ones in our solar system. The people who inhabit Tela are called Daus. I am one of them.

"Always there had been peace in our universe. Then, a few years ago, the Lundars—they come from Virna—struck at us; conquered us. They have made us their slaves."

"But how?" demanded Wolf, his eyes cold and calculating. "They don't look too tough to me—"

THE other smiled sadly. "We knew little of war," he explained. "Besides, the Lundars had discovered a source of power so great as to be beyond belief. They discovered that the third planet of our system, Ra, was nothing but a great lump of a radioactive ore, which their scientists converted into pure energy practically without processing. They broadcast this power to their war fleet. We were beaten."

"So that's it." The buccaneer chief was sober. "No hope at all?"

"None. Until recently the Princess Meersa and I kept up a guerilla fight. But we were captured, and now these"—he nodded toward his fellow-Daus—"the last of our fighters, lie here in prison, awaiting transfer to Ra."

"Why Ra?"

"Always the Lundars need men for Ra. The workers there die from contact with the ore within six months. A horrible death, in agony. That is why Ra is used as a penal station."

"I see." Wolf frowned. And, after a pause: "What's your name, friend?"

"Orcutt."

"Well, Orcutt, have you got any ideas on where the *Ghost* might be? It's a big ship—big enough to carry all my men, and yours beside, so there ought not to be too many landing fields big enough to take it."

The other meditated for a moment.

"I think I have it," he declared at last. "Probably the Lundars have put it in the great central port."

"Where's that?"

"It is close to the Tribunal Hall. A half-hour through the tube."

"Will you guide us there?"

Orcutt nodded. "Yes, gladly. But"—he shook his head—"it is little use to talk about it. This prison is strong, and the Lundars are many. We could never get away."

Wolf Stone's eyes flashed blue flame. His thin face was hard.

"The prison isn't built that can hold my band." he clipped. He turned. "Ivar!"

"Here, Chief." The big mate moved close.

The leader's eyes were once again probing the prison. Taking in every detail. Searching for the smallest weakness.

"We'll have to go out the same way we came in," he decided at last in a low voice.

"Back past them cops?" His aide looked shocked. "Chief, them Lunkers, or whatever you call 'em, ain't wearin' guns for ornaments."

The buccaneer leader gripped one of Ivar's arms. "Of course they're not ornaments. They've got them to shoot unruly prisoners like us with. But do you remember the break we made at Horosha, on Mercury?"

A slow grin spread across the mate's ugly face. "Do I remember!" he smirked. "Whoee! And I'll bet everyone on Mercury does, too."

Then, turning to Orcutt:

"How about it, buddy? Do these dopes have any kind of an alarm system to warn 'em that birds like us is trying to flyaway?"

It took the young Dau a minute to digest the Jupiterian's unique phrasing of the question. Then he nodded.

"Yes. Any break in the walls, or any serious tampering with the bars, sounds a warning bell. That brings all the guards rushing out the door on the other side of the corridor, there. And since we're behind bars, they can kill us at their leisure." He sighed. "One of the bans tried to pry loose one of the wall plates. They burned him down before he could even get his fingers under it."

Ivar's bullet head nodded solemnly. "You called the turn, Wolf," he acknowledged. "They were fishing for sharks with a minnow net when they put us in here."

"Then what are we waiting for?" Wolf Stone demanded, his eyes very hard and bright. "Let's go…"

CHAPTER TWO
Flight for Freedom

THE stage was set in less than ten minutes. Two heavily thewed Saturnians ripped apart one of the strap-metal bunks, which lined the rear of the bullpen as easily as if it had been made of tinfoil.

A lizard man directed them at their task. When they were finished, he selected the straightest of the metal slats; had them break it in half. They did the job in such a manner that the Martian had a three-foot strip of heavy metal, pointed at one end. A very ugly sort of sword, for close-quarter stabbing.

Slat in hand, the lizard man walked over to a position close beside the bars separating the big cell from the corridor, and a few feet to the right of the point at which the door from the police squad room opened into the opposite side of the hall.

Five Saturnians now gathered at the other end of the bullpen, several feet to the left of the squad room door. They gripped one of the bars between them and the hallway.

"Stop them!" cried Orcutt. "Don't you understand, Wolf Stone? If they try to pull out that bar, the Lundar guards will shoot them down—"

"Let me worry about it," the raider snapped.

The others of the band were hastily equipping themselves with the remainder of the bunk slats.

Wolf Stone surveyed the scene through narrowed eyes: The Martian, at one end of the cell. The Saturnians, at the other. The remainder of his men, crouched eagerly in the background.

"Ready?"

The lizard man waved his pointed metal slat. "Ai!"

"Uhhh!" chorused the Saturnians. "Now!"

As one man, the Saturnians heaved. Their great muscles rippled and swelled. Their powerful backs seemed to spread with the strain. But the bar held firm.

Again they heaved, and again. Their horrible, hairy faces twisted with effort. They bared their fangs—

Then, suddenly, like a sapling in the wind, the bar bent inward. Tore loose from its settings.

A hell of clanging bells broke out. The squad room door burst open. A twelve-foot Lundar guard rushed into the corridor, gun in hand. His eyes fastened on the Saturnians.

But before he could so much as raise his weapon, the lizard man behind him, at the other end of the bullpen, hurled the three-foot metal slat. Like a silver streak, it sped through the air, whistling a song of death. The point drove home between the Lundar's shoulders in a hammer-blow. He staggered. Bent at the knees. Slumped forward, blocking the doorway.

The same instant the bar gave way, another Martian sprang. He leaped across the Saturnians. Through the gap in the bars. Across the hall. His scaly reptilian claw snatched the gun from the Lundar's dying hand. He blazed away with it, criss-crossing the squad room with streaks of purple light. The Lundars' cries changed from roars of rage to screams of panic.

The rest of the *Ghost's* wild crew were swarming out of the cell and into the hall.

THROUGH the doorway they surged, makeshift weapons swinging, faces contorted with grimaces of hate. This was work they knew how to do—killer's work; work for Wolf Stone's raiders.

Wolf himself was in the forefront. He hurled himself forward, drove a long strip of slatting into the pit of a staggering Lundar's stomach with all his might.

"Prisons, Ivar!" he bellowed. "They've not yet made the prison that will hold us!"

And beside him, the mate, a captured light-gun in hand, roared back a savage affirmation.

Close on their former captors' heels, the raiders rushed down the tunnel to the subway station.

But, from one corner of his eye, Wolf caught a glimpse of Orcutt, the Dau, jerking open another of the squad room's doors and disappearing through it. The Earthman stopped short.

"What's he up to?" he muttered half-aloud. "He's supposed to guide us."

For the fraction of a second Wolf hesitated. Then he raced in pursuit of the young Dau.

A long corridor stretched beyond the door through which Orcutt had disappeared. But there was no sign of him. Wolf sped along it. At its end loomed the shadowy black well of a descending staircase. Noiseless as a wraith, the space raider slipped down it.

The stairs ended in a dimly lighted chamber. A door was set in its far side. Before it, Orcutt blasted savagely at the lock with a Lundar light gun. Silently hugging the shadows, Wolf watched him work.

A moment later the lock gave way. The heavy portal swung open.

"Orcutt..." cried a voice from the blackness beyond.

"Meersa!"

The next instant the lithe, slender figure of a girl stumbled out of the darkness and into the stocky young Dau's arms. Her pale, lovely face was radiant with joy.

"How did you do it?" she gasped. "Oh, Orcutt, how did you get away?"

Orcutt's voice was choked with emotion. "Meersa, my princess! You are safe!" Then: "All our men are free, saved from the Lundars by strange creatures from another universe. Already they have destroyed the guard squad, and—"

"Look out!"

The girl's voice was shrill with fear. She jerked free from the man's arms. Her hand shot out, whipped the light gun from his grasp. She snapped a shaft of purple brilliance toward the stairs. It missed Wolf's head by inches.

The buccaneer lunged forward in a somersaulting fall that carried him all the way across the chamber. He landed in a heap in a far corner. Took in the scene with one glance.

The Dau princess still stood tense by the door, gun raised, eyes wide with excitement. Orcutt half-crouched close beside her, paralyzed with shock.

And, looming on the stairs like a drunken Frankenstein, tottered the monster figure of a Lundar guard. His red eyes were staring, face twisted in awful surprise, hands clutching at a black cavern that yawned in the center of his chest, where the bolt of light had struck. Even as Wolf watched, the giant went limp. Plunged to the floor.

Orcutt's eyes flashed across the corpse to where the Earthman sprawled.

"Wolf Stone." he gasped. "How came you here?"

SLOWLY, the buccaneer got to his feet. His blue eyes were centered on the girl, Meersa, drawn to her as filings to a magnet. Ignoring the young Dau's query, he approached her.

"You saved my life," he said gruffly.

Tela's princess gazed up at his lean face. "I cannot claim credit," she said. "I was thinking of myself, and of Orcutt. I saw the Lundar even before I realized you were in the shadows. My shooting was instinctive."

Then, to Orcutt:

"But who is this man? Whence does he come? I do not recognize him, nor his race."

"He is Wolf Stone," the stocky Dau explained. "He is the one of whom I told you—the creature from another universe who released us all from the Lundars' grasp—"

But the space raider's eyes still were riveted on the girl. You saved my life," he repeated. "One step more and that thing"— he jerked his head toward the corpse—"would have killed me. He must have played dead when my men passed through the squad room, then followed me when I came after Orcutt."

"It is nothing," murmured the Princess Meersa.

A grim smile rippled over Wolf's thin lips.

"Nothing?" he mocked. "My life is nothing? Princess, to me it is everything. I have fought my way through a sea of blood to preserve it.

"But now it is mine no longer. You have saved it, so it is yours."

There was a fierce intensity in his tone that made the girl's breath come faster. She dropped her eyes.

"Please—" she whispered. "I ask no credit—"

The Earthman said: "My life is yours. I must redeem it."

"No—"

"Yes." Blue fire danced in the raider's eyes. "I'll buy back my life on my own terms." His jaw was hard. "Hear me, Princess. From this moment on, your fight is my fight. The Lundars have been your enemies; now they are mine. I'll stand with you 'til they are but a memory. It is a promise, Princess, Wolf Stone's promise!"

Orcutt said: "We are wasting time. Soon the alarm will spread. More of the Lundars will be rushed here to seize us."

His words seemed to break the Earthman's spell. He turned.

"Right. Come on."

Together, the three hurried up the stairs and down the corridor to the squad room. Halfway there they met Ivar, running toward them.

"We been hunting for you like a Plutonian for trouble," he greeted his chief. "We was scared one of them zombies had sunk a ax in the back of your neck."

"Not yet," Wolf grinned. "What's doing?"

An unpleasant, mirthless smile lit up the big mate's face. "They tried to run," he chuckled. "Them big dopes tried to run. But we shot faster."

A FEW minutes later they were entering the subway station. Raiders and Daus alike were milling about nervously. Lundar bodies littered the platform. Several others were strewn along the tracks, some of them burned beyond recognition through falling against third rails apparently similar to those used by early Earth underground systems.

Meersa saw them. "Oh!" she choked.

Ivar shrugged. "Don't worry about 'em. They was out to kill us, only we got 'em first."

"That isn't what she means," burst out Orcutt. "Don't you see? Anything falling across those rails causes a short circuit. It warns Rsk's headquarters that something's wrong up here. They'll send out a squad to find out."

"Then it's time we got moving," snapped Wolf.

"Yes," spoke up Meersa. "We can go down the tracks. The last station is in the foothills. From it we can escape into the mountains. We can hide there."

"No," said Wolf Stone.

"What?"

"No, we're not going to hide." The buccaneer's blue eyes danced with a daredevil light. "That's what the Lundars expect us to try. If we do it, they can hunt us down at their leisure."

"But what else can we do?" demanded Orcutt, puzzled.

Wolf laughed harshly.

"We can attack!" he cried. "We can do the thing they least expect. We can put *them* on the defensive."

"You mean—?"

"We're goin' back. Back to the central port you told me about, where the *Ghost's* stored." He turned to his mate. "Ivar!"

"Sure, Chief!"

"Scout around. See if there's any way we can get back to that shiny mausoleum of Rsk's—"

The big man from Jupiter grinned like a delirious sculptor's gargoyle. "We already done it, Chief," he announced. "Some of them goons run off down that siding"—he jerked one of his four brawny arms toward a narrow passage into which a spur of track ran—"but me and a few of the boys lighted their way for 'em." He slapped the light gun in his belt in grim significance.

"When we caught up to 'em," he then concluded, "we saw they'd been trying to make it to that little train we come down on. It's there now."

Wolf's eyes flashed back to Orcutt. "Can you pilot the things?"

The Dau nodded. "My men can."

"All right. Let's go."

Daus and raiders alike swarmed aboard the underground train. The men of Tela no longer looked broken and dejected. The swashbuckling, reckless spirit of the buccaneers had communicated itself to them. They moved now with hands up, eyes glowing with excitement.

Half a dozen lizard men scrambled onto the train's head end, their scaly claws gripping weapons. A Dau, directed by Orcutt, took the controls. The vehicle jerked forward. Gained speed. Careened down the blackness of the tunnel, back toward Rsk's Tribunal Hall.

Wolf Stone turned to Meersa. "What is Rsk? Sort of a military governor?"

"No." The Dau princess shook her lovely head. "He is the gar—that is, the king, the ruler—of all the Lundars—"

"But I thought they came from another planet—"

"They do," Meersa nodded. "From Virna. But it is far out from our sun. Tela, our own planet, is more centrally located. That is why the Lundars have made it their capitol, the place from which they rule our whole solar system."

"Fine rulers." snarled Wolf. "The way they treated us—"

THE princess of Tela smiled sadly. "They treat my people worse," she said. "The Lundars believe themselves to be a superior race. The more so since the happenstance of their planet's development resulted in them being twice our size. They see in my people only serfs—dirt under their feet. They kill ruthlessly. They delight in torture. In the glory of their power, they see might as the only right—"

Wolf Stone's eyes were dark. "I've seen such before," he said. "If it had not been for their likes, I might never have come to Tela." There was an almost cruel twist to his lips. "Well, if force is the only language they can understand, that's the one we'll talk to them. And believe me, princess, my men and I are fluent in it…"

"Chief! Trouble!"

It was big Ivar's harsh voice. The Earthman sprang to his side.

They were coming into a familiar station—the station below Rsk's great Tribunal Hall. The platform thronged with Lundars. All were armed.

"It's the party being sent down to see what is wrong at the prison." shouted Orcutt.

"Keep moving, then!" roared Wolf. "Don't stop here. Get on up to the next station before they start shooting."

The train picked up speed. But barely in time. Light guns already were out and blasting at them.

"They're coming, chief!" Ivar bellowed. "They got another train. They're on our tails."

Wolf caught Orcutt's arm. "Hurry up! Get more speed out of this thing!"

"It is going as fast as it can now."

The raider chief turned. He could see the glowing headlight of the pursuing train, speeding along directly behind them.

"Where's the next station?"

"Just beyond the central port."

"How long before we hit it?"

"Another minute. No more."

"Men!" Wolf roared.

The babble of strange tongues ceased as if it had been cut off with a knife.

"In another forty seconds we stop. I want every man out onto the platform and ready for a fight before the wheels quit spinning."

The Earthman spun back on Orcutt. "Does this outfit have a reverse?"

The Dau nodded. "Yes."

"Then tell your man to put it at full speed back the second we stop."

"You mean—?" The stocky man of Tela stared back at the glowing headlight of the pursuing train. Then: "Of course, they are on the same track—"

"Right." Wolf smiled grimly. "I told you my side played rough. These Lundars are in for trouble."

The next instant they pitched forward, thrown off balance by the sudden braking of the vehicle.

"Come on!" Wolf roared.

LIKE magic, the train emptied. Wolf shoved Orcutt and Meersa onto the platform. By the time his own feet hit, the cars were, backing faster and faster.

From down the tracks came the scream of brakes.

Ivar said: "Them zombies must of catched on, huh, chief?"

But the Lundars were too late. Already their train was within feet of the other. No force could halt it in time.

Crash!

A hideous cacophony of rending metal and Lundar shrieks shredded the darkness. Then blue flame leaped in balls about the wreck.

"The electricity!" came Princess Meersa's horrified gasp. "It has passed the insulators… It kills them all. Nothing could live through it."

"Come on!" snapped Wolf. "We've got to get to the *Ghost.*"

They raced up a long stairway, out of the subway and toward Tela's surface.

Ahead, from the first of the raiders, came sudden shouts of tumult.

"Hurry up!"

Wolf ran ahead. He came out into a strange world of purple and gleaming metal. Buildings of unfamiliar architecture towered all about. It was the raider's first glimpse of this world's outdoors.

But he had no time to stand and contemplate. His men were fighting savagely against the onslaught of a Lundar troop. More of the giants were pouring into the street from a dozen directions.

Orcutt rushed out of the subway tunnel. Wolf caught his arm.

"Where's the port?"

"There. Back there." The Dau pointed toward a monstrous metal heap towering behind them.

'The Earthman shouted orders. His crew began falling back, fighting their way toward the structure. They had only one advantage: surrounded as they were by the giant Lundars, they could fire at will with their captured light guns; but their enemies could not, for fear of hitting each other.

With the desperation of the already damned, they hacked their way. A dozen times the force of numbers almost overwhelmed them. Once a Lundar caught Wolf's shoulder, almost broke it before the Earthman could shoot his way free.

And then, miraculously, they were within the gigantic central port before their enemies realized their goal. The great metal doors slid shut. The raiders swarmed to take defensive posts beside the entrances. Others hunted down the handful of Lundars trapped within.

But Wolf and his chief aides raced through the monster building's corridors. Hurried into elevators. Rushed to where the *Ghost* stood empty and idle.

Brief minutes of inspection told the story. Their great, black pirate ship was safe. Ready to take off down the long runway at a moment's notice.

"The jackpot!" whooped the irrepressible Ivar. "The old girl's as frisky as a *zotar* in mating season. All we got to do is let her roll—"

"Then you had better do it!" retorted a lizard man who had just sped up. His lidless eyes sought Wolf. "We are holding them below," he reported tersely. "But they are many. Soon they will break through. We must take off quickly if we are to live to fight again."

But Wolf's face was tense and desperate. He was staring off down the metal runway, and through the exit port beyond.

"How did the *Ghost* get in here?" he grated to Orcutt.

The Dau's face showed bewilderment. "How? Why, through the entrance port at the other end of the building. You take off down this runway—"

"No."

"What—?"

"That building's in the way. The big one down there." The buccaneer leader's blue eyes were sharp with worry.

"But, surely—"

"Your ships must be smaller and more maneuverable than ours. The *Ghost's* too big ever to make it. And we can't turn it around to go out the same way it came in. It's too big for that, too."

"Then what—?"

Wolf Stone drew a deep breath. "Nothing. Orcutt, we're trapped. We fought our way here, and now—we can't get out. The Lundars have got us!"

CHAPTER THREE
Enter Znz

THERE was a long moment of stunned silence.

At last Princess Meersa spoke. Desperation was in her voice.

"We can't fail now. Not after we've gotten this far. There must be some way—"

Wolf smiled bleakly, ran long, nervous fingers through his Indian-black hair.

"Sure," he agreed, "there's a way. There always is. The only question is: can we find it in time, before those devils outside break through and cut our throats?"

Ivar's voice broke in like an exclamation point. "Wolf!"

The raider chief spun about. His big Jupiterian mate had gone off with the lizard man in charge of the defenses. Now he was running back.

"We ain't got enough to hold 'em, Wolf," he gasped out. "Them palefaces has gotten in. They keep coming, just like a bunch of them black beetles on Mercury, that even fire can't stop."

"They've gotten in!" The other's lean face was drawn and tense. "What—"

"The boys have fallen back. We're holding 'em in this section, on the second level. But that ain't going to be long. They keep coming, Wolf. They just keep coming—"

Like a caged lion, Wolf paced the floor. Then:

"Where's Moko, our scientist?"

"Down below," grunted the mate. "The last I saw of him, he was playing tit-tat-toe on one of them zombies with a light gun."

"Get him up here, then. And send along a bunch of Venusians."

"You got an idea, chief?"

"Half a one. Hurry up!"

Seconds later the stooped figure of the raiders' Uranian scientist hurried down the runway toward the spot where Meersa, Orcutt, and Wolf stood beside the *Ghost*. Close on his heels were half a dozen of the weird-appearing mechanics of the crew, eight-armed Venusians.

"Yes, yes?" sputtered Moko, the purple beard that covered the top half of his face twitched nervously, while his bright little eyes darted this way and that. "What is it, Wolf? What do you want?"

"We've got to get the *Ghost* out of here," the leader reported tersely. "That building down there is in the way, though. So we'll have to turn the ship around and go out the same way we came in."

"Yes, yes. Go on."

"To turn the ship, we'll have to tear the guts out of this whole section of the port. Can we do it?"

The Uranian scurried off down the runway. He shot glances from one side of the monster hangar to the other. Glanced hurriedly at the structural network overhead. For perhaps a minute he studied the problem. At last he returned to Wolf.

"No. Can't do it."

"What do you mean, can't? Why not?"

"Hmph!" The little scientist snorted. "Can't you see? Cut out enough of the bracing to give space to turn the *Ghost* around and the whole place would cave in. Architecture reminds me of Pluto. All part of a unit. Pull out one piece and the whole thing falls down."

THE buccaneer chief bit his thin lip hard. "We've got to figure an angle. We've got to get out—fast!"

"Chief!" Again Ivar rushed up. "We've had to fall back to the third level. And now they're bringing up some big outfits that look like artillery to me—"

"Atom projectors—" choked Orcutt. "They throw bolts of energy. Nothing can withstand them. But that they do such damage, and that the Lundars are so proud of this great port building, no doubt they would have used them before. One blast, from the biggest projectors, and this whole place would be a mass of smouldering ashes."

"Maybe we could do some blasting, too, chief." Ivar suggested. He waved one of his four brawny arms at the *Ghost*. "Why don't we use our proton cannons on that there building that's in our way? We could blow it from here to Neptune-"

"Nonsense." broke in Moko the Uranian peevishly. "At close range, yes. But that building's too far off. We wouldn't even damage it. Not from here."

"Wolf Stone!" cried Meersa. "I have an idea!"

"What is it?"

"Why don't we abandon your ship? We can escape in the Lundars' space freighters—"

"We cannot, Meersa," interrupted Orcutt. "They no longer dock freighters here. Only a fleet of little aerocars do they keep here. They are good only on Tela, you know. They cannot go beyond the stratosphere."

Little Moko, the scientist, skittered about nervously.

"If only we had explosives…" he fretted. "We could load the aerocars and pilot them by radio over to that building. That would get it out of the way."

Wolf Stone stopped short. A flash of sudden enthusiasm— of hope—drove the worry from his blue eyes.

"That's it!" he cried.

"No. No." Moko was adamant. "We haven't any explosives, Wolf. If we had, yes. But we haven't."

"We don't need explosives—"

A lizard man rushed up. "More than a few minutes more we cannot hold, Wolf Stone." he reported, his cold voice tense.

"Already the Lundars have inflicted heavy losses. Now they hurl bolts of power at us. We cannot retreat much farther—"

The lean pirate chief turned on Ivar.

"Quick!" he snapped harshly. "Line up every aerocar in the place for a fast flight to that building."

He whirled to Moko.

"Get the radio directional apparatus ready. Hurry!"

"But we haven't any explosives—"

"I know it. Do as I say now. You can argue later."

Then, to the Martian:

"And you: get the men ready for a fast run up here. Tell them to board the *Ghost* and prepare for action."

Tela's princess, close beside him, stared up in puzzlement. "I do not understand," she said.

But the *Ghost's* commander paid her no heed. A dynamo of energy, blue eyes afire, he snapped curt orders right and left to the crew members who now hurried about him.

IVAR panted up, sweat pouring from every pore. "I got 'em ready, chief. Orcutt's turning 'em on now. They got no power plants, you know. Pick their juice right out of the air from this Ra place. So I ain't had to worry about that."

"Right." Wheeling, the other ran up the *Ghost's* ladder to where Moko was working. "How much longer?"

"Nearly ready now," fluttered the Uranian, brushing wisps of purple beard back out of his eyes. "Another minute. That's all. Be all ready to pilot those aerocars wherever you want them to go. But no explosives. It's silly, without explosives—"

Wolf ran back out of the space ship. "Ivar!"

"Here, chief!"

"Get below. The second the men get a breathing spell, have them abandon their posts. Get them up here. Every last man of them."

"You bet, chief. On the nose." The big mate lumbered off.

Wolf hesitated long enough to flash Meersa a thin smile.

"If you know any prayers," he told her, "now's the time to say 'em. If my scheme works, we'll live to harass the Lundars from one end of your solar system to the other. If it doesn't— well, lady, you'll never live to worry about it."

"But what—"

Before the buccaneer could answer, the *Ghost's* crew came across the port floor in a rush. Into the ship they poured.

"Moko...have you got that radio directional apparatus ready?"

"Yes, yes. All ready. But you can't—"

"Ivar!"

From the rear of the motley band swarming into the *Ghost* came the mate's ready, "Here, chief!"

"All aboard?"

"Yeah. All on. But we got to do whatever we're going to fast. Them Loonies'll catch on that we ain't down there fighting in another second—"

"Close the hatches—" Wolf shouted. "Prepare for flight..."

The space ship's sound detectors caught the tumult of Lundar shouts from the abandoned barricades below.

"See," growled Ivar. "They're wise already. No dust on their tails, may they rot..."

Wolf Stone's cold blue eyes stabbed at Moko the Uranian.

"Take off those aerocars." he clipped. "Set them down on the roof-field of that old building that's in our way. In regular formation, as if they were loaded to the ailerons with men."

"But what good—"

"Do it!" Wolf roared. "Don't argue! Do it now!" His voice was like a lash of flame.

The Uranian hunched over the maze of radio equipment. He twisted dials, threw levers.

INTO the *Ghost's* telescreen—sighted on the building, which loomed black against the sky at the far end of the runway— came myriad forms, like squads of tiny insects maneuvering. They moved toward the building.

Through the sound detectors came the Lundars' wild shrieks of rage.

The next instant half a dozen of the little aerocars burst in mid-flight like clay pigeons.

"The atom-projectors!" cried Orcutt. "They're not afraid to use them now."

The raider chief paid him no heed. "Now!" he cried. "Hurry, Moko! Bring them down on the roof."

Like swallows, the aerocars swooped down, precisely obedient to the little scientist's manipulations of the radio directional equipment. One after another, they landed.

"Now... Watch—" Wolf grated.

Almost at the same moment, it happened.

Like a house of cards crumpling, one corner of the big building that barred the *Ghost's* way vanished. Faster, faster, it disintegrated. Its weather-scarred surface caved under an invisible bombardment. Then, with a rending crash, one whole side gave way. The entire structure tottered perilously for a moment. Hung on the verge of complete collapse. Let go at last. Crumbled into a heap of smouldering ashes.

"Take off!" roared Wolf Stone. "Set a course for outer space!"

His words were still echoing through the control room's confines as the great ship blasted down the runway, out of the port, and off over Tela's sprawling capital city.

Ivar, eyes still bulging with amazement, stared at his commander.

"I don't get it, chief," he complained dolefully. "One minute that big shanty was as solid as the mountains of Jupiter. The next, it was caving in like it was made of fog and soapsuds."

Wolf smiled thinly. "It's just as I told you, Ivar," he explained. "There's always a way out, if you can only think of it. This time, it was aerocars and atom projectors. Moko gave me the idea when he spoke of blasting that building with explosives—only we didn't have any.

"Then it hit me. I saw that if we flew that fleet of aerocars over to the other building, the Lundars would blast the whole place out of the way. Especially since it was an old building. They'd already gotten so desperate they were using small projectors even back there in the central port, which they certainly *didn't* want to destroy."

"Uh…I don't get it yet, chief. Why'd they go off their nuts about them empty hacks?"

"Of ALL the thick-headed apes…" the leader exploded. "Ivar, you Jupiterian jackass, the Lundars thought we were in those aerocars. That's why I timed the take-off so carefully. What would you think, if someone you were fighting disappeared, and a minute later a ship just around the corner took off? We were all here, in the *Ghost*, with the hatches closed. So the Lundars figured—just like anyone would—that we were running for it."

"But how could you be sure?" broke in Meersa. "How could you know that they'd destroy that building, instead of storming it, the way they did this one?"

The Earthman shrugged. There was a reckless twist to the corners of his mouth.

"I couldn't know," he answered. "It was just a gamble that worked. Just a putting of myself in the Lundars' place—figuring how I'd feel if someone I thought I'd trapped made a clean get-away. It made them jittery. They wanted to swat us, hard and fast. And the quickest way was to blow the whole building out of the universe—"

The lovely Dau princess nodded.

"Yes. I can see it, now. You are a clever man, Wolf Stone—"

The buccaneer nodded, in his turn. "I'd be lying if I denied it," he told her grimly. "The only reason I'm alive is that I've been clever enough to dodge a hundred traps. When a space pirate keeps his head on his shoulders, it's proof he's clever."

"And now—?"

The raider's eyes were almost dreamy.

"Now," he answered, "we give Rsk, gar of the Lundars, the worst headache he's had since he quit making mud pies and throwing snowballs.

"Already," he went on, grinning wolfishly and running his thin fingers through the heavy black hair that crowned his head, "we've disturbed his peace of mind a bit, I imagine. One day after we recover consciousness, we stage a successful mass jailbreak." He chuckled. "That's the stuff nervous breakdowns are made of."

"What do we do first?" Orcutt demanded enthusiastically.

"We establish a base. Some spot we can work from. A place we can fortify—"

"I know just the place!" cried the Dau. "It is a small asteroid, a satellite of Suorz. The Lundars fortified it during their war against the primitives who inhabit Suorz, but by now they must have withdrawn all but a small garrison. If we capture it, we can use the long-range atom projectors they mounted there to fight them off—"

"Just the place!"

A Saturnian shambled in.

"Big space freighter off our bow," he mumbled in the strange, guttural speech of his people. "The Daus say it's a Lundar ship."

Again Wolf grinned. "Sorry, friends," he announced, "but this means changing our plans. We'll have to postpone setting up a base until we can clean up a business transaction—something involving the cargo of a Lundar freighter."

THEY were mad days, those that followed. Days that saw the *Ghost* cruising from one end of the solar system to the other, hovering over every Lundar like a hawk above a coopful of chickens. Days when Rsk's battle cruisers swarmed the spaceways in vain, searching for an enemy they could never find. Days that brought terror to the farthest Lundar outpost, and fear of raiders even to Virna, the giants' home planet.

Days in which Wolf Stone showed why Interplanetary Police reward posters had termed him the most dangerous pirate who ever roamed the void.

One lightning attack gave the buccaneers the asteroid Orcutt had described. The *Ghost's* proton cannons blasted three-quarters of the garrison to oblivion even before the Lundars realized they were being attacked, and the rest went down under a single swift, savage rush. From that day on, the raiders had an almost impregnable base from which to operate.

But Wolf Stone was not satisfied.

"Yes," he told Meersa, Orcutt, and Ivar one day after a particularly successful attack on Tela, "we're causing a lot of trouble. But that isn't enough. The Lundars are getting better organized, now. They're tightening their patrols. Hemming us in a little closer all the time. Sooner or later the day will come when we can't send the *Ghost* out." He paced the floor, his face grim with worry. "We've got to figure out something bigger. Something that will paralyze the Lundars—"

"But every raid brings us new recruits from the oppressed peoples," Meersa objected. "We know that they would revolt if they could—"

"But they can't!" Wolf snapped back savagely. "They want to, but as long as the Lundars have the arms, no one can fight back. And our raids are not much beyond nuisance value, now." He shook his head. "No. We're wearing ourselves out, yet we haven't really accomplished anything when it comes to cracking Rsk's regime."

"Oh, but—"

The princess's sentence was never finished. A Martian lizard man burst into the room, cutting her off.

"Lundar cruiser approaching, sir!" he snapped to Wolf. "They're flashing truce signals."

"Truce?" The buccaneer frowned. "That doesn't make sense."

"But that's what they're doing, sir. It looks like they're coming in for a landing."

There was a long moment of tense silence. Then:

"Put one of the Daus who talks Lundar on the interspacial radio. Have him warn them that they'll be blown out of the sky the instant they try anything funny."

"Yes, sir."

THE Martian hurried away, while Wolf crossed the room to a telescreen.

Sure enough, a Lundar ship was bearing down on them.

"It's one of Rsk's personal cruisers!" cried Orcutt excitedly.

Meersa's enthusiasm equaled that of her stocky aide. "Maybe he wants to arrange a peace..." she suggested breathlessly. "Maybe his nerves are cracking—"

"No." Wolf shook his head. "It couldn't be that. After all, what peace terms can you make with a pirate? Certainly he's not going to agree to free all the planets he's seized. Yet that's obviously the only solution, so far as we're concerned."

"They're landing, chief." Ivar broke in. "Some guy is getting out. Must be a big shot, too. He's wearing enough medals to build an aerocar."

Again the door opened, and the lizard man stepped in.

"A visitor, sir," he told the leader. "An envoy from the Lundars."

"Not Rsk, is it?" demanded Wolf.

"No, sir. It's his aide, the sub-gar."

"The sub-gar!" gasped Meersa and Orcutt in chorus. There was horror in their eyes.

Then:

"Not even Rsk would be so foolish as to send the sub-gar," whispered Meersa.

"No!" choked Orcutt. "Even the Lundars hate him as a fiend. He is the one who has had charge of 'pacifying' all subject races. He wallows in blood. No man in all Tela would treat with him. It cannot be him—not the sub-gar."

"We'll soon find out." Wolf turned to the Martian. "What's his name?"

But before the lizard man could answer, another voice cut in. It was a strange voice, deep and rumbling, and there was something in it that sent little chills of stark terror racing up and down every spine in the room.

"I am the sub-gar," the voice said, from beyond the doorway. "I, Znz!"

CHAPTER FOUR
Double-Cross

THE raider chief stared up at the giant Lundar who stalked through the entrance.

"We've met before," he remarked.

"Have we?" asked the sub-gar in a puzzled tone. "I did not know—"

"Your memory's short," retorted Wolf. "Indeed, Znz, we have met before. You stood with Rsk when my men and I were dragged before him. In fact"—he smiled thinly—"you suggested that we be sent to die in the pits of Ra, your power planet."

"Yeah," grunted Ivar, moving relentlessly forward like a great, four-armed gorilla. "That wasn't nice. I hear them pits is no honeymoon cruise. But you wanted to send us to 'em—"

Wolf caught one of the Jupiterian's arms. "Forget it," he snapped. "This is no time to pick a fight."

The Lundar's white face twisted in a grimace apparently intended to represent a smile.

"My thanks," he said. "I should hate to have to hurt one of your men—"

"No thanks are necessary," the other snapped. "My reason for stopping Ivar was that you must have had some reason for coming here. I want to know what it is."

The sub-gar's red eyes shot glances at Meersa and Orcutt.

"What I have to say is for your ears, alone," he murmured. "These others too much knowledge might hurt them. It would be unwise—"

For a long moment the Earthman eyed the Lundar narrowly. Then he turned to Ivar. "Take our friends outside," he ordered.

The Dau princess flared.

"I will not be ordered about!" she cried. "You are not my superior—"

Wolf's eyes bored holes in hers. "I am in command here," he snapped. "You will leave. Now."

"You can't—" Orcutt began.

"Ivar!"

The big mate shot his chief a single rebellious glance, then turned on the two Daus.

"Quit stalling." he snarled. "You heard him. Get moving. You ain't snoring; quit acting like you was asleep." He herded the still-protesting pair from the room.

The pirate leader turned back to Znz.

"All right," he clipped, "I've done what you wanted. Now talk—"

The sub-gar smirked. He said: "You and I have much in common, Wolf Stone."

"Have we?" The Earthman's lips were compressed to a thin, dangerous line. "Perhaps you'd better explain what you mean."

"Of course." A moment's pause. Then: "I mean, Wolf Stone, that we both do as we like. When we see something we want, we take it. Both of us are ruthless; that is why we have risen to power."

The space raider eyed Znz warily. "Go on. Tell me what this is all leading up to."

Again the smile-grimace. The Lundar hunched forward confidentially.

"TOGETHER we can rule a universe!" he cried dramatically.

"How would you like that, my friend? To loot whole worlds, instead of single freighters. To rule planets, instead of one space ship's crew... To have nations bowing before you—women fighting for your favor—"

"A pretty picture," Wolf agreed. "You have a good imagination, Znz—"

"But it is more than imagination!" the Lundar said tensely. "Together, Wolf Stone, you and I can make that vision reality. We can rule this solar system. We can make every living creature pay tribute for even being allowed to breathe—"

The Earthman bared his teeth in a mirthless smile.

"And my allies, the Daus?" he demanded. "Where do they fit in?"

Znz smiled back. "They do not," he said. "They are weak fools, meant to be ruled by men like us." A moment's pause. "Surely a leader like you would not let such slaves stand in his way. Surely you can see—"

"I am a believer in expediency," Wolf retorted. "I'm the original opportunist. I make my alliances to fit my needs. So far, my best bet—my only one, in fact—has been the Daus. But if you can show me something better—" He gazed reflectively at the Lundar.

The sub-gar chuckled. It was like the sound of an avalanche of ice.

"I told you we were two of a kind!" he cried. "We see things alike."

"But so far," the Earthman reminded him, "there has been nothing to see. Or did you come all the way here from Tela in order to talk over my personal philosophy?"

"No. I came here in order to get your aid. Together, we can overthrow Rsk—"

Wolf nodded. "Yes. So I gathered. But how do we do it? That's the only question that counts."

The sub-gar took a deep breath.

"Your success against us has laid the groundwork," he explained. "There have been murmurings against Rsk.

"Now I have taken advantage of them. I have persuaded certain of our garrison commanders to join in a revolt. With you to aid us, it cannot but succeed."

"How does it work?" the Earthman demanded. Interest was written across his lean face.

"You know of Ra?"

"Your power planet? Yes. We thought about raiding it, but finally decided it was too strongly guarded."

"That is right," agreed the sub-gar. "Without help, you could do nothing."

"That is why we need each other. I have friends on Ra. They will revolt as you attack. You will seize Ra!"

"Then what?"

"Then you will turn off the power which is broadcast from Ra to every corner of the solar system. It will cripple Rsk. The atom projectors—the light guns—the space ships—the whole mechanism of our civilization—will be paralyzed."

"I see." Wolf ran his fingers thoughtfully through his thick black hair. "And what do you do?"

A SMIRK distorted the Lundar's face.

"I have long been gathering weapons," he explained, a crafty light in his red eyes. "Old weapons, all of them. Weapons, which do not use the power, broadcast from Ra. I have space ships, too, and aerocars, and the flying suits which we used in the days before Ra's conquest.

"With them, my men can seize Tela, Virna, and Suorz alike. Rsk will be helpless without power—and before he realizes what is happening, he will be dead!"

"I see."

"Well, what about it?" The sub-gar leaned forward eagerly. "Is it not a good plan? Can you find its flaw? Will you join me?"

The Earthman considered long and carefully. At last his cold blue eyes met the bloody orbs of the Lundar.

"I'm your man," he said grimly. "We'll do the job together, and to hell with whoever gets in the way!"

Znz exploded to his feet from the table on which he had been resting his twelve-foot frame.

"I knew you would see it!" he cried. "I knew that the loot of a universe would tempt you!"

"As it does you," the buccaneer commented bleakly. "I don't have any illusions about your purity of heart, Znz."

"Of course not," chuckled the pale giant. "Did I not tell you we were of the same cut? We both look after ourselves first." A wild spasm of laughter shook him: "Ah, Rsk. How he'll love it when he finds that this 'inspection tour' I'm making of our patrols actually is the preliminary step to his death. He'll wish he'd never treated me like a second-rate *starbo* before he's through, the *chitza!*"

"No doubt," agreed Wolf, somewhat caustically. "But now, if you can stop gloating, let's get down to details."

More than an hour passed before the plans for Ra's invasion and conquest were completed. When they were done, Znz once again embarked. His space cruiser moved off into the void, while Wolf hurried off to find Ivar.

The big Jupiterian was talking to Orcutt when the Earthman strode up.

"Some act you put on, Chief," the mate greeted him. "You sure sold that Loonie a bill of goods. Me and Orcutt and Meersa was listening outside the door."

A thin-lipped smile crossed Wolf's face. "Yes," he admitted, "it was quite a bill of goods, as you say. Quite a different one than Friend Znz is expecting, anyhow. He'll find that a double-cross can work two ways."

"You mean," said Orcutt, the Dau, "that you are not betraying my princess and me?"

The look the raider shot him was as bleak as a January gale.

"Do you think so little of Wolf Stone's word as that?" he clipped. "Have I shown myself to be the kind of a dog that would turn on those who saved his life, for the sake of loot?"

The young Dau's eyes dropped. "I—I did not mean it so," he stammered in embarrassment. "It was only that you call yourself a pirate...and your words were so convincing when you spoke to Znz..."

"I BEEN putting the dope on the right track, Chief," Ivar broke in. "I gave him the whole works—all about how you turned pirate just because the Interplanetary Federation over on our side of the void was pulling a Hitler—"

"You'd do better to keep your mouth shut!" barked the commander, his own face suddenly pale at this mention of the past. He turned on Orcutt. "Well, are you satisfied now? Or do you still think I've sold you out—"

"Please—I am sorry—"

"All right." A pause. "It's pretty obvious what Znz wants to do. He needs us to capture Ra for him, but you can stake your life that he's not planning on letting us stay with him at the finish. Some place or other along the line, he'll see to it that we're wiped out, leaving him to run things to suit himself."

"Sure, Chief. We ain't supposed to have a chance. He'd sell his own mother to Saturn. It sticks out like a *podor's* horns."

"Right. And it's no compliment to his intelligence that he thinks I'd fall for it."

Orcutt, his composure now recovered, broke in: "But what do you plan to do? You agreed to his plan, so—"

"We're going to give that traitor a surprise," the other answered. "We'll capture Ra for him, sure. But after we've got it—"

"That's something else, huh, Chief?" snorted Ivar.

"It is indeed. This is the break we've been waiting for, and we'll make the most of it. Alone, we could never defeat the Lundars. But with Znz to aid us for the time being-well, on Earth we have a saying, 'divide and conquer'." Then: "There's a lot to do. I've got to get to work."

Orcutt caught his arm as he turned to go.

"Could you...first...speak to Meersa?" the young Dau asked.

156

"Meersa? Why? What about?"

The princess' stocky aide shifted his feet uneasily.

"She was very sure you had betrayed us," he explained finally. "She would not even stay. She ran off before you had finished talking to Znz."

"Where'd she go?"

"I do not know. To her quarters, probably... If you would see her..."

"Sure. Come on."

Together, the pair walked across the grounds of the garrison post to the little building in which the princess of Tela lived. Wolf knocked on the door.

"Meersa! I want to see you."

An echoing silence was his only answer.

"Meersa! Open up!"

Still silence.

The spaceman jerked open the door. He and Orcutt pushed into the Dau princess' room.

There was no one there.

"EMPTY!" exclaimed Orcutt. "Certainly looks that way," admitted the Earthman. His blue eyes probed every corner of the chamber. He prowled about restlessly.

"I don't like it," he said at last. "I've got a feeling something's wrong."

Orcutt, the Dau, nodded acquiescence. "I, also." His broad, white face looked strained.

Wolf turned sharply.

"Probably we're seeing ghosts," he announced. "Let's go have a look around the rest of the garrison before we get worried about things."

Together, he and Meersa's stocky young aide hurried off across the grounds. From post to post they went, searching, inquiring, looking into every likely and unlikely place of the asteroid's garrison for the girl. But an hour's investigation brought no results.

"Where can she be?" Orcutt fretted nervously. "I cannot understand."

Wolf frowned. "Just what did she say when she left?" he quizzed.

"She was very angry. At me, because I could not believe that you were betraying us, as well as at you. She swore she would no longer keep the company of traitors to Tela's cause. Then she ran out."

"Would she have been foolish enough to try to leave?" the Earthman pondered. "No matter how sore she was, would she…"

"Let us go to the landing port," proposed Orcutt. "There we have not yet looked. And the men there will at least know whether any ship has taken off—"

"Right. Come on."

But again they were doomed to meet with disappointment. The Venusian in charge of the transport unit shook his head.

"I am sorry, my commander," he reported, "but no ship has taken off since morning."

"None at all?"

"None—that is, except the Lundar cruiser that brought Znz hither."

"The Lundar cruiser—" exclaimed Orcutt. "Wolf Stone, could Meersa have been taken by them?"

The Venusian interrupted. "It is the Princess Meersa you seek, my commander?"

"Yes, of course," Wolf snapped. "Have you seen her? Has she been here—"

"Yes. She arrived two hours ago, and went out among the ships. I have not seen her since—"

"Wolf!" cried Orcutt. "Could the Lundars have seized her? Could they have taken her away?"

The Earthman's blue eyes blazed. "I can't believe it," he snapped. "Their cruiser was under guard every minute. But if they did—if somehow they got Meersa on board—ah, what a master stroke! "

THE Venusian who had charge of the port was pushing buzzer buttons with all eight arms.

"I shall have every inch of the port, and every ship, searched immediately, my commander," he declared. "If the princess is here, she will be found, or—"

"No," snapped Wolf. "We can't waste time on a search now. If that girl's in Znz' hands, every minute we delay means that she'll be that much farther away."

"But what can we do?" protested Orcutt feverishly. "What else is there to try?"

The raider chief's lean brown face was grim. His voice was tight-clipped, pregnant with suppressed emotion.

"We'll follow!" he snapped. "The *Ghost* can outrun anything in the void. By morning, we'll have caught up with Znz. We'll force him to heave to for a search—"

"But your plans—your arrangements for joining forces with him to dethrone Rsk and seize the solar system—"

The Earthman shoved back an unruly lock of jet-black hair. His lips were even thinner than usual. "If necessary," he rapped curtly, "those plans will have to go by the board. Meersa's life is worth more than any of them. Once, she saved me. Now, I'll protect her, no matter how much it costs us."

He turned on the Venusian. "Order a skeleton crew onto the *Ghost*. We take off in ten minutes."

They bettered the time he specified. Seven minutes from the moment he spoke, the great space ship was in the air, hurtling out of the asteroid's atmosphere and on across interstellar space in the wake of the Lundar cruiser. Ten hours later they were abreast their prey.

A Venusian interspacial radioman came to Wolf.

"The Lundars want to know why we are pursuing them," he reported.

"Answer that we're looking for the Princess Meersa, and that we intend to come alongside and search their ship for her," the Earthman answered.

A minute later the Venusian looked up from his instruments again.

"Znz says they do not know what you are talking about, but that they have no intention of letting us or anyone else search them."

Wolf Stone's blue eyes flashed fire. He leaned forward like an animated threat.

"Tell them they can take their choice—be searched, or be blown to hell," he snapped savagely. "Tell them that if they think they can fight off the *Ghost*, they're welcome to try it. But that they shouldn't be surprised if they never see their home port again."

And, to a Martian gunner's mate who stood at his elbow:

"Man the proton cannons! Open fire at your own discretion, at the first sign of anything suspicious."

The Venusian said: "Znz protests, but says he will submit to temporarily superior force. You may go aboard the cruiser."

THE sub-gar's red eyes were seething with anger as Wolf and a searching party boarded the Lundar ship through an airlock.

"You put great stock by this Dau princess, Wolf Stone," he said, in a voice that shook with rage. "Too much stock. I wonder if perhaps you were not lying when you agreed to join me. If perhaps you do not mean to uphold the cause of the Daus against me—to betray me if you get the chance."

The Earthman turned on him, lean jaw hard.

"Let's not make any mistakes, Znz," he bit off coldly. "You don't trust me, and I don't trust you. We've got no reasons to, and you know it as well as I do.

"The reason we're joining forces is because we both want loot and power. Alone, we're weak. Together, we can tear a universe to pieces. So, for the time being, our interests are parallel, and either of us would be a fool to betray the other until we've gotten what we want.

"As far as the Princess Meersa is concerned, she's mine. I want her. I intend to have her—as a woman, not as a princess. And no one—sub-gar or not, ally or not—is going to stand in my way on that.

"For that matter, I wouldn't let you get away with stealing a cross-eyed *starbo*, let alone kidnapping one of my people. You'd think it proved I was afraid of you, and that I could be pushed around." He grinned wolfishly. "And neither of those ideas is correct, you know, Znz, so you might as well put up with this search gracefully."

The Lundar had regained his self-control.

"Very well, Wolf Stone," he purred. "If I must, I must." Then, smirking: "Though you should be able to do better for yourself—with our whole solar system to choose from—than to take up with a Dau princess, a woman of a subject race."

"We'll leave my taste out of it," Wolf rapped curtly.

A lizard man entered Znz' cabin. He saluted Wolf.

"The Princess Meersa is not aboard this ship, sir," he reported in the chill, lisping voice characteristic of his race. "We have searched every inch of it, from stem to stern, but we find no traces of her."

"Right." The raider chief turned back to Znz. "My apologies. It seems that my suspicions were not well-founded."

Again the Lundar smirked. "No apologies are necessary," he declared with a ring of complete insincerity. "Such errors are quite understandable in a man of your violent temperament. We shall think no more—"

"Commander!"

It was the Venusian radioman. He rushed into the cabin waving a sheet of paper.

"Well?"

"The princess has been found, my commander. I have just received word of it from the asteroid garrison."

"Where was she?"

"She was hiding in a small torpedo ship, sir. Before anyone could stop her, she took off."

"A torpedo ship?" Wolf's brows knitted. "But with a limited range like they have—"

"There is only one place she could go, my commander. Only one planet close enough. By now, no doubt, she is fast approaching the wilderness of Suorz."

CHAPTER FIVE
Attack on Ra

ORCUTT, the Dau, said: "But aren't you going to search for her, at least? We cannot go away to Ra, leaving her helpless and alone on Suorz." His broad face was lined with worry.

Wolf Stone paused in his personal supervision of the *Ghost's* loading.

"Sorry, Orcutt," he said, "but I'm afraid that's just what we're going to have to do. Znz already suspects things aren't exactly what they seem; and if we give him time, he may get so jumpy he'll act on fear, instead of sticking to a logical appreciation of his own best interests. So I figure our best bet is to act now—fast! Once we get Ra—"

"But Meersa..." the stocky young Dau protested. "She may be in danger. Even now, she may be dead—"

"Sorry, Orcutt."

"Then I won't go!"

Wolf gazed at him. "And what do you propose to do?" he asked.

"I'll take a torpedo ship and go after her myself," the Dau flared. "I'll show her there's one man who cares more for her, herself, than for any dream of conquest—"

"Orcutt, Orcutt!" the Earthman reproached. "Can't you see it doesn't make sense? What Meersa wants is freedom for the Daus, not personal safety. Furthermore, she's well able to take care of herself on Suorz. There's only three groups there—the Lundars, whom she'll be careful to avoid; the Bans, who are so primitive and dull-witted they're not at all likely to hurt her; and a colony of your own people, the Daus, who'll go out of their way to watch over her."

"But Suorz is a wilderness," the other persisted stubbornly. "Millions of square miles of the worst kind of country, with nothing inhabiting most of it but *quirsts* and *peens*." He glared at Wolf. "Have you ever seen a *quirst?* We've got some in the great interplanetary zoo back on Tela. They're like snakes with arms. Let them even breathe on you and you will welcome death. They are the most venomous creatures in the whole solar system. They strike without warning, for the sheer love of killing. Think of poor Meersa, there on Suorz, with them!" He shuddered.

"I wish I could agree with you," answered Wolf quietly, "but I can't. I'm as anxious as you are to protect Meersa—you saw how quickly I ordered the *Ghost* into action when I thought the Lundars had her; but right now, I think she's safe. And if she isn't, frankly, it's because she's acted like a stubborn kid instead of a woman with the responsibilities of a princess."

"Well," sulked Orcutt, "I still won't go to Ra. Meersa means more—"

"All right, then; go wandering off across Suorz in a torpedo ship if you want to!" snapped the Earthman, his patience exhausted. "Do whatever you want to. But I've got work to do, so leave me alone."

Turning on his heel, he again gave his full attention to the *Ghost's* loading.

AN HOUR later Orcutt, in a tiny, two-man torpedo ship, took off for Suorz.

It was nearly two days after the *Ghost's* return from intercepting the Lundar cruiser, however, before Wolf completed preparations for the invasion of Ra.

"It looks good, chief," Ivar grunted as they finally blasted off from their asteroid base. "The old girl's in swell shape. And them new atom projectors the Daus showed us how to build— say, them is going to be quite a shock for the Loonies on Ra.

Imagine being able to blow a bunch of guys to kingdom come with their own power!"

Wolf nodded. "It's a sweet set-up, all right, Ivar. If there's a flaw to it, I haven't been able to find it."

The Venusian in charge of the radio room came in. "A code message from Znz, my commander," he reported. "He says all details are ready. We are to attack on signal, and at the positions indicated previously."

"Right." Wolf turned back to his mate. "Full speed ahead, Ivar. The quicker we get there, the quicker we can go into action."

But despite the *Ghost's* best speed, the trip to the remote little power planet took more than a week. Then, at last, they were hanging in interstellar space above it.

"There it stands, Ivar," Wolf said softly, his eyes gleaming, lean face tense. "That little globe we see below us is the key to the Lundar civilization. Smash it, and we've smashed them."

The big mate nodded. "Yeah. Without the power they send out from there, them Loonies are up a creek." A pause. "What angle we working, chief? How do we hit 'em?"

"We come in on a beam," the buccaneer leader answered. "By following it, we can get close enough to blast their defenses. Znz' followers are immobilizing the atom-projectors in that area."

"Uhhh," grunted his aide.

Wolf eyed him narrowly. "What's the trouble, Ivar? You don't sound too enthusiastic."

"Uhhh…"

"Go ahead. Tell me. What is it?"

The big Jupiterian raised one of his four brawny arms, scratched the back of his bull neck reflectively.

"Chief," he demanded at last, very solemnly, "do you figure this Znz Loonie is on the up-and-up? Or is he throwing a loose peg, like a Uranian gambler in a *horo* game?"

"I see what you're getting at, all right." Wolf nodded slowly. "And the answer is: no, I don't trust him as far as I could throw him—which isn't far, considering that he's twelve feet tall and not too easy tossing."

"I DON'T like that beam business, chief," his mate announced grimly. "What I mean is, maybe it's supposed to guide us in, and then again, maybe it ain't. Maybe it's just supposed to put us right where them zombies down on Ra can blow us clear out of the solar system, without no chance at all of missing."

The raider chief frowned. "I don't think that's it, Ivar," he said. "After all, Znz has got to have somebody to cut off the power, or his uprisings on Virna and Tele are going to go haywire."

"Has he?"

"What do you mean?" The Earthman eyed the burly man from Jupiter with an air of puzzlement.

"Well—" Ivar gnawed his lip, struggling to find words to fit his meaning— "well, it's like this. If I was Znz, I sure never would deal you in."

"How would you get around it?"

"Look, chief, if Znz has got a bunch of his own guys on Ra, why don't they just bust up the outfit that broadcasts the power? It'd be lots easier than knocking off a whole batch of atom-projector batteries, wouldn't it?" He thumped one big fist into the palm of another hand for emphasis. "You ask me, chief, that Znz lug is playing you for a sap. He ain't planning to cut you in on nothing. All he wants to do is kill us all off, so we ain't going to be messing around while he's got his revolution on the fire."

There was a long moment of silence, broken only by the creak of Wolf Stone's footsteps as he paced the floor. His thin lips were compressed tightly against his teeth, and his blue eyes were narrowed and hard.

"It adds up," he said at last. "God knows it adds up, Ivar. Smashing the power broadcast equipment would stop Rsk just as thoroughly as letting us capture Ra—and with a lot less danger of trouble, too. By blasting us, he'd kill two birds with one, stone—"

The Earthman stopped in mid-sentence. He whirled to face his mate.

"You win, Ivar." he snapped. "From here on out, we play it alone."

A grin like a half-moon pasted itself on the big Jupiterian's face.

"Swell, chief—" he grunted. "What's our angle now? Do we still try to knock off Ra?"

The other nodded. "Sure. With this solar system out of power, we hold all the cards."

"How do we work it?"

A reckless, daredevil grin twisted the corners of the Earthman's mouth.

"We attack, Ivar. We attack, just like we promised to. Only instead of letting Znz name the place and time, we'll choose our own."

"Where and when, chief?"

"The place? The other side of Ra, Ivar. And the time? Why, Ivar,"—and the raider's eyes flashed fire—"the time is as fast as we can get there."

TENSE minutes followed. Minutes of tumult, as the *Ghost* changed course and the indicators moved forward to "full speed ahead." Alert minutes, with every piece of gear being checked and rechecked. But, above all, joyous, exciting minutes—the minutes in which fighting men from a dozen worlds girded themselves again for battle.

"We'll come in fast," Wolf rapped to his aides. "With luck, we'll be on top of those devils down below before they realize what's up. When we land—well, we'll let that take care of itself."

The next instant they plunged Ra-ward.

Centered in the telescreen, the little power planet grew larger by the second. It filled the ground glass, developed details of geography, broke into all the multitudinous landscapes that go to make up a world.

"Them Loonies ain't wise yet, chief," Ivar grunted from his place beside Wolf. "They ain't opened up on us at all yet. And we're nearly down, too."

As if to contradict him, the *Ghost* suddenly rocked from side to side, like a kite in a thunderstorm.

"Ai! That was close." the mate gasped.

But before the words were out of his mouth, a great splash of light flared on Ra's surface.

"Good shooting!" exclaimed Wolf. "They missed us with their first barrage, but we got them with ours. We're one up on them."

Other batteries now joined the battle. The bolts from their atom projectors tore at the pirate ship. With deadly aim, the *Ghost's* gunners gave them back good measure.

Then, suddenly, the ship was through the worst of the hail of death.

"That's the trouble with them atom projectors," Ivar thundered into Wolf's ear. "They may be all right for long range stuff, but when you get up close, where you have to place your shots fast, give me a proton cannon any day."

Already, these latter were taking a terrific toll of Ra's defenders. Every time a battery on the ground opened fire, the awful shafts of energy belched from the *Ghost*, smashing the mightiest defenses as if they were cardboard.

"We are landing, my commander!" cried the Venusian at the helm.

"We've blasted the last of the batteries on this side of the planet." echoed the lizard man who headed the gunners. "We can use it for a base."

A minute later the great space ship was sliding to a precarious stop amid the ruins of the silenced atom projectors.

BUT now came a new menace. From all sides, in rushed mobile, tank-like units, while overhead tiny torpedo ships and armed aerocars whistled down to harass the invaders with a storm of deadly energy-bolts.

"No wonder this place got the reputation of being impregnable," grated Wolf. "They've got every known defense on hand and ready for action. Except for surprising them, we wouldn't have gotten within a hundred miles of the ground before we'd have been blasted to nothing."

"What do we do now, chief?" Ivar demanded a bit anxiously. "Some of them outfits is getting a little too close for comfort. They'll have our range in a minute, and then—wham!"

"Yes. I know." The other's face was taut with strain. He paced the floor. "The trouble is, we haven't got the man-power to take over the rest of the planet. And as long as the Lundars are here, we're penned up like chickens in a coop."

"Yeah," grunted Ivar dourly. "What's more, they got the mines and the energy, and we ain't. And we sure could use some."

"The mines!"

"Huh? What did you say, chief?" But Wolf was shouting for the Venusian navigator-pilot. In a moment the eight-armed creature came running up.

"Yes, my commander?"

"We're making a run for the head of the mine-shafts." snapped the Earthman. "Prepare for a take-off."

Then, to the Martian gunners' mate:

"Get ready for a fight. A real one!"

Ivar caught at his arm.

"What's got into you, chief?" he demanded. "Them mines is where the Loonies will have the heaviest artillery they got. If we go there—"

Wolf turned on him.

"We've got to do it!" he grated. "We can't retreat now— they'd nail us before we got ten miles out. That means we've got to stay here and win."

"Well," growled the Jupiterian dubiously, "maybe the shock'll lick 'em. But I doubt it."

The buccaneer leader flashed him a brief grin.

"If we can get those mine shafts, we'll have more than shock to use to lick 'em," he retorted.

The next instant the *Ghost* was again in the air. Like a monster skyrocket, it blazed across Ra's sky, its mighty proton cannons carving a path for it through the heart of the Lundar defenses.

Then it stumbled in mid-flight like a stricken hawk. Almost fell.

"We are hit, sir!" shouted the Martian gunners' mate. "They have torn a bad gash near our stern."

"Our power plant is crippled, my commander." called out a Venusian.

"Can we make it to the mines?"

"Limping, perhaps; but we shall be an easy target."

"Hear that, you gunners?" Wolf roared. "We're bogged down. That means you've got to wipe out every Lundar battery within range. If one gets a clear shot at us now—"

A crippled bird, the *Ghost* lurched onward. Then:

"Up ahead, chief. The mine shafts!"

"Crash in to a landing! We'll make our fight around the shafts!"

WITH an avalanche roar of rending metal and cracking rock, the *Ghost* came in. Almost in the shadow of the great slag piles that surrounded the mine heads, she lurched to a stop.

"The mines! Run for them!"

The *Ghost* belched forth men. Weapons in hand, they stormed across the yard that separated their battered ship from the looming tipples.

A dozen Lundars sprang up to oppose them, light guns spearing forth purple rays. They went down like ten-pins beneath the wave of raiders.

"The slag piles!" roared Wolf. "Occupy them! Make them our barricades!"

Another party of Lundars, the crew of an atom-projector battery, burst into view. A swarm of buccaneers rushed to meet them. Wolf was in the forefront.

"I want a prisoner—" he shouted as he dropped the first of the enemy party with a deadly Earth ray gun. "Save me one prisoner!"

Then there was no time for talking. Not even for shouting orders. The pirates were grappling hand-to-hand with their giant foes. Making up for small stature with a savagery the paste-colored ogres could not withstand.

A moment that was eternity, and the job was done. The Lundars who had guarded the mine shafts were dead, all but one of them. And he lay prostrate, panting, held down by Ivar and two mighty-thewed Saturnians, his lymph-like blood oozing from a shoulder wound where one of the Saturnians had bitten him in a dozen places.

Back on the slag piles, the rest of the *Ghost's* crew were sweating their lives' away, dragging proton cannons and atom projectors to makeshift emplacements.

Wolf Stone bent over the captive Lundar.

"Where are the slaves?" he questioned fiercely. "Where are the Daus, and the Bans, and all the rest of the poor devils you've got working these hell-holes?"

The giant tried to spit in the Earthman's face.

The raider chief gestured peremptorily. One of the Saturnians—both of his horrible, hairy heads grinning ghoulishly—braced himself. He gripped the Lundar's arm in a grasp of iron. The massive muscles of his back and shoulders swelled. With one jerk he snapped the prisoner's arm.

A cry of agony burst from the Lundar's white lips. Sweat stood out on his forehead.

"I want to know! Where are the slaves?" Wolf's voice had the ring of doom itself.

The Saturnian caught the Lundar's other arm.

"No!" shrieked the prisoner. "They are in the first shaft. Their quarters are at its foot. All are there—"

"That's all I want to know." snapped the Earthman. "Come on, men!" He ran toward the mine the Lundar had indicated.

The two Saturnians shambled after him. Only Ivar hesitated. He pulled his ray gun. Leveled it at the prisoner's head. His finger tightened on the trigger...

WOLF and the Saturnians scrambled into a monster mine car, weapons in hand, alert for trickery. Deep into the bowels of Ra they plum meted. Down...down...down...until at last the car reached bottom. A narrow tunnel led still further into the depths. They followed it, tense and expectant, straining their eyes in the dim light.

Then two Lundar guards loomed before them, light guns in hand.

The first Wolf dropped with a single ray gun blast. The Saturnians sprang like tigers onto the other, disdaining even to use their weapons, so great was their love of battle.

Beyond them loomed a great metal door. The buccaneer leader blasted at its lock. Watched the metal fuse and twist and drop away.

The door swung open.

The sight beyond would have chilled the heart of Ivan the Terrible, himself.

For a moment the three raiders stood in stunned silence, staring at a sight the like of which not one of them had ever seen before.

"And I thought Neptune's salt pits were the closest I would ever be to hell." Wolf whispered at last.

Then he and the Saturnians were moving forward, among the awful, wasted, rotted forms of the men who gave this universe its power. Strong men, they had been. And some of them—the younger, and those but recently brought here—still were. But most of them lay like putrefying corpses, too stupefied to move.

"Men!" shouted Wolf in the dialect of the Daus. "You're free—free to fight the Lundars again!"

171

At first they would not, could not, believe him. Precious minutes dragged by while he explained, argued, debated. Then, all at once, it seemed to dawn on them. Like a human tidal wave, they came alive. Poured out of their prison and down the tunnel to where the mine cars waited.

Ivar was at the head of the shaft.

"Chief! What you been doing?" he cried. "We need you bad. Them Loonies is too much for us. They got us outnumbered, and they're pushing us back."

"They don't outnumber us any more, Ivar." Wolf answered grimly. "Break out some guns…I've brought us a battalion from hell!"

CHAPTER SIX
When Worlds Collide

HATE turned to action is an awful thing. It took the slaves from the mines of Ra less than two days to slash and blast and stab their way to complete control of the little power planet. Free again, armed by the raiders, no Lundar could withstand them as they charged forward in one mad rush after another, welcoming death as a friend come to release them from the lingering agony of an existence poisoned by the awful radioactivity of the metal they had been mining.

In a week, Venusian repairmen had the *Ghost* nearly ready for flight again. Others of the crew were exploring every inch of Ra's surface, while Moko, the Uranian scientist, was beside himself with joy at the opportunity to investigate the system of power broadcasting developed by the Lundars.

"Simple. Really it is. Quite simple," he assured Wolf. "Electrolytic process. The ore's so pure that all they have to do is to shoot the current through it. Turns it into pure energy. They pick it up as vibrations. Broadcast it. The receivers reconvert the waves into power."

"I think we ought to turn a little of it into power right now, then," grunted Ivar, who stood beside the commander. "That big goon, Znz, ain't wasting time, you can bet your neck on that. By now he's probably got Rsk run short-legged. Believe me, chief, we ought to turn on enough power for interspacial radio work, anyhow. Then we could get an angle on what's cooking."

But Wolf Stone shook his head.

"No," he said. "Not until the *Ghost* is ready to cruise again. Give the Lundars power, and they might sweep down on us before we could stop them. And with the *Ghost* crippled, what could we send out to stop them? Nothing but the bunch of broken-down atomic-powered freighters we captured from the Lundars here.

"No." He shook his head again. "We'd be trapped here, with nothing but ground defenses. And if we could break those defenses once, someone else could do it again. We're better off to leave the power turned off completely."

"You don't make sense, chief," his mate protested. "If anyone started to attack us, we could snap the power off, and they'd be left drifting—"

"Maybe. Or maybe the power would let them get just close enough to come the rest of the way with some other kind of energy. Sorry, Ivar. But the power stays turned off. We're raiders. We need a ship under our feet. Not to be trapped on a stinking little planet like this one."

"Can't stay too long, though," broke in Moko. "Got to leave soon."

"Why?"

The Uranian smoothed the purple beard that covered the upper half of his face.

"Too dangerous," he retorted. "This whole planet's one big lump of radioactivity. You've seen the sores. The ones on the Daus and Bans, and all the rest who worked in the mines. They rot away. It's the ore. Whole planet's that way—"

"You mean—"

"Get us too, if we stay too long. Got to take off. Quick—"

The door burst open. A Martian rushed in.

"There is a ship approaching, sir!" he exclaimed. "We sighted it but a moment ago."

"A SHIP?" Wolf went tense. "But how—?"

"They had space ships in this solar system before them Loonies knocked off Ra and got all worked up over the broadcast power idea, chief," Ivar reminded him. "Maybe there's still some of them old outfits kicking around, huh? Like them freighters we found here."

"Could be. But we better take a look."

They hurried outside.

"It is still too far out to be visible to the naked eye, sir," the Martian reported. "We saw it through the telescreen magnifier on board the *Ghost*."

"Right. We'll go on board. See to it that our proton cannon are ready."

A Venusian was manipulating the telescreen.

"It is larger now, my commander," he announced. "The ship comes closer."

Together, Wolf and Ivar studied the image in the screen.

"Something new to me, chief," grunted the big mate, frowning. "I never seen one like it before."

"Neither have I." And, to the Venusian: "Get one of the Daus in here. Maybe he'll recognize it."

A minute later one of the natives of Tela was beside them.

"Yes," he agreed after a moment's scrutiny, "I have seen such ships before. But it is old. Very old. It is one of those my people used before the Lundar conquest, powered by atomic energy."

Eyes narrowed, Wolf stared at the image of the approaching ship. It was limping along slowly, a far cry from the swift, efficient vessels of the Lundars, let alone the *Ghost*.

"There's nothing to do but let it come," he decided finally. "But we'll keep it covered every inch of the way. At the first sign of trouble—we drop it."

Slowly, the ship hovering above Ra came closer and closer, lumbering laboriously onward toward the face of the planet. On the ground, the *Ghost's* crew and the freed slaves waited on the alert, tensely expectant.

"Watch it, men!" Wolf rapped, his blue eyes glued to the now-visible space ship. "We're taking no more chances than we have to. If you see anything suspicious, fire at will!"

Still nothing untoward happened. The ship settled clumsily. Maneuvered for a favorable position. At last landed with a thump in a valley between two of the great slag piles.

One of the *Ghost's* buccaneers, an Earthman, started to approach it.

"Back!" roared Wolf. "Wait 'til they open up!"

As if prompted by his words, the forward hatchway of the ship swung outward. A familiar figure appeared.

"Orcutt!"

"YES. Orcutt!" The young Dau swung to the ground. His broad face was gaunt. Great, dark hollows shadowed his eyes. He stumbled as he came forward to meet the raiders. Wolf caught his arm.

"Orcutt! What is it? Tell me!"

"It's...Meersa."

"Meersa! What's happened to her?"

"The Lundars...they've got her."

"The Lundars!"

"Znz has her. He captured her on Suorz."

Wolf's bronzed face was nearly as pale as that of the Dau princess' aide.

"Start at the beginning," he commanded sharply. "Tell me exactly what happened."

"Well...I went to Suorz in the torpedo ship, just as I'd planned to. And I even found Meersa. She was all right, just as you said she'd be.

"We went in our ships to the Dau colony on Suorz. I could not quite convince Meersa that you did not mean to betray her.

She wanted to stir up a revolt in the colony, drive the Lundar garrison off the planet. That's how we happened to fix up this ship." He jerked his head in the direction of the vessel in which he had come.

"Yes. But go on: How'd the Lundars happen to capture you?"

"It was Znz. You had hardly left your asteroid base for the raid on Ra, Wolf Stone, when he appeared. Already he was betraying you, even before—"

"I can imagine that without any trouble. But what about Meersa?"

The young Dau tried to force a smile; failed miserably.

"Znz' men were wearing the flying suits the Lundars used for short trips before they got Ra's power," he continued. "They came down on us one night while Meersa and I were reconnoitering in space between Suorz and the asteroid. We were in our torpedo ships. We each had a helper from the Dau colony—only one, though; those little ships will accommodate only two men."

"But what about the Lundars?"

"They came upon us suddenly. Their bodies, in the flying suits, were as long as our ships. They threatened us, by gestures; that they would burn open our cockpits unless we obeyed them. That would have meant instant death, so we were forced to go with them to where a Lundar cruiser was stationed. Znz, also, was there. He told us he had sent you to your destruction, and that he intended to keep us prisoners.

"Then the power went off. When it did not come back on, Znz was furious. I knew then that you had not been killed— that somehow you had captured Ra. So when a chance came for me to escape, I took it, even though I was not able to save Meersa. I went to the Dau colony and got this old freighter and a crew. We came here at top speed, hoping you could somehow save Meersa."

"With Znz stranded on Suorz?" Wolf smiled grimly. "I wouldn't be surprised if I could, Orcutt. We've got the *Ghost* nearly ready to fly again—"

"But Znz is not stranded," the young Dau broke in excitedly.

"HE'S not stranded? What do you mean?"

"Did I not tell you? The cruiser he came to Suorz in was equipped for flight without the broadcast power. Even before I escaped, he was making his plans to leave for Virna, the home planet of the Lundars. His cruiser took off but a few hours before we did—"

"Virna!" Wolf's face was pale again as he exploded the name. "If he ever gets there, there's no chance at all of rescuing Meersa. It's beyond the realm of possibility that we could invade the Lundars' own planet and still save her alive."

"Of course. But could you not catch his cruiser before he reaches Virna? The *Ghost* is fast, and, without broadcast power, Znz' own ship is even slower than the one in which I came here—"

"It wouldn't do any good. He'd put in at Tela, instead, if he saw we were going to catch him."

"But he cannot put in at Tela!" Orcutt cried excitedly. "There his revolt failed, and Rsk is still in control. It would be as much as his life was worth to land there!"

There was a gleam of excitement in Wolf's eyes, too, now.

"Maybe we can make it, then," he snapped. "Virna's a long way from Suorz." He turned. "Moko!"

The little Uranian stepped forward. "Yes, yes?"

"Give us some fast calculations. Can we catch Znz before he gets to Virna?"

The scientist whipped out a scratchpad. "Have to figure distance—speed—route," he chattered, and began firing questions at Orcutt.

For nearly a minute, then, he calculated and checked. At last he glanced up.

"No. Can't be done. You'd be two days late. Maybe more. *Ghost's* not ready to blast off, anyhow—"

"But there must be some way—"

"Maybe. But I don't know it. Have to go faster than any ship I've ever seen."

The pirate commander turned on his heel. "Come on, Orcutt. You, too, Ivar. I've got some thinking to do."

Two hours later, he was still racking his brain for a way out. For the fiftieth time he halted in front of the great celestial chart which hung on the wall of the *Ghost's* control room.

"There must be a way." he fumed. "There's always a way—"

"—if you can find it," grunted Ivar dourly. "Yeah, you've said that a million times, Chief. But this time there just ain't none. Not unless you can rock this whole damned chunk of mud off its orbit on a special trip to Virna—"

The lean Earthman stopped dead in his tracks.

"That's it!" he exclaimed.

"Huh? What you saying, Chief? What is it?"

"You hit it, Ivar! You called the turn!" And, to Orcutt: "Get Moko, Quick! Every minute counts now."

THE young Dau dashed out. Seconds later he was back, dragging with him the sputtering little Uranian.

Get your hands off me, you *podor!*" screamed the purple bearded scientist, struggling to escape. "Let me alone—!"

"Moko!"

The Uranian stopped short in his tirade, caught by the bite of Wolf Stone's voice.

"Yes, yes?"

"Moko, Znz isn't going to get to Virna!" he blazed. "We're going to beat him to the draw—"

"'Have to show me—"

"I will. Moko, we're going to knock Virna out of the sky—"

"*What?*"

"You said this planet is practically a solid lump of radioactive ore, didn't you?"

"Yes, but—"

"All right, then." There was a triumphant fire in the Earthman's cold blue eyes. "We're going to throw Ra at Virna, faster than any missile ever went before. So fast that it'll hit Virna before Znz' cruiser can possibly get there—"

"But—how—you can't—no—it isn't possible—"

"It is possible. Look here." Wolf's lean forefinger traced a course across the celestial chart. "See, Znz won't ever pass between Ra and Virna, so we don't need to worry about that angle."

"But you cannot move a planet from its orbit—"

"We can this one." The buccaneer chief's face was flushed with sudden enthusiasm. The cords of his neck were taut with excitement.

"Don't you see?" he rushed on. "Ra is one big lump of radioactivity—of energy, waiting to be released. If we let enough of that power go, and in the right direction, we'll blast Ra through space like a comet with an automatic pilot—"

"But how? Can't control it—can't—"

"Yes. We can. At least, we can if you were right about the energy being released through electrolysis."

"Of course I was right!" the little scientist bristled.

"All right, then. First, you'll have to calculate the angle of approach, and all—you know, just how to aim Ra in order to hit Virna—"

"Yes. Yes. Go on." The Uranian's eyes were bright with interest.

"Then we'll put two of the old freighters the Lundars left here out in space. We'll anchor them exactly according to your calculations. Then, by passing a powerful bolt of electricity between them, we'll electrolyze one whole side of the planet."

"You mean touch the whole works off like a skyrocket, Chief?" burst out Ivar in stark, staring amazement. "Blow it all the way across the solar system, and into Virna—"

"Yes. That's it. Exactly."

"NO. You can't." It was Moko. He shook his head vigorously. "No. Not enough power. Where could you get a bolt that strong?"

"From Ra."

"What?"

"From Ra." Wolf's eyes were gleaming. "Don't you see? This planet has been supplying a whole universe with power. Can you imagine what that would mean, if we threw the broadcast system on full force, and all channeled into one great bolt, passing between those two freighters—?"

A look of awe transfused the scientist's purple-bearded face.

"Wolf Stone," he whispered, "you are mad. But also, I think, you are a genius. Your plan is insane, but it might work. We shall try it!"

Every man who could lift a hand worked in the mad hours that followed. In minutes, almost, the *Ghost's* repairs were completed, and the great raider ship was ready to take the air. The former Lundar slaves were loaded onto the freighters captured in the occupation of Ra and sent far out into space, to give them time to put sufficient distance between themselves and the doomed power planet.

The raiders, meanwhile; equipped two of the freighters with the electrical apparatus necessary for them to serve as the poles in the great experiment. Ra's power broadcasting system was changed to allow completely automatic operation.

At last Moko the Uranian came out of his quarters.

"The figures," he told Wolf. "All checked. Ready to go. Here"—he shoved forward a slip of paper—"positions for the freighters. Go ahead. Any time you say."

"Right." The raider chief roared orders, watched the two-pole vessels rumble aloft.

A last-minute check-up. Then:

"Prepare to blast off. We pick up the men on the freighters, then head for outer space."

The jerk of the take-off came and went. The slowing to allow the men delegated to placing the freighters to come back aboard the *Ghost.* The long run to a safe position. And then—

"Are we ready?"

Little Moko checked a chronometer.

"Another minute and the position will be exactly right for intercepting Virna's orbit," he said. "Everything's automatic. We don't do anything."

Silence. Tense, pregnant silence. With every eye focused on the telescreen, where the image of Ra hung centered and motionless.

Baroom!

Even here, a thousand miles out in space, they could feel the concussion. One side of Ra suddenly glowed red, then white, in the telescreen. The next instant the power planet was moving. Leaving its orbit. Slashing a new path across the void. Gaining speed. Faster, faster, faster, with flame seething in its wake like the blast from a rocket's tail.

"It is going…" whispered Orcutt, the Dau, his voice shaking.

On and on it went, out through the eternal night of interstellar space. On and on, toward Virna, drawn there like a needle to a magnet.

"Full speed ahead," commanded Wolf Stone. "We've still got to find Znz."

"Full speed ahead!" echoed Ivar thunderously. "Get moving, you lugs! The chief says blast! "

THREE days later the pinpoint of light that was Virna suddenly leaped to match-head size. An instant later it went out entirely.

"They're gone!" choked Orcutt, the Dau, tautly. "The Lundars' home planet is gone!"

But it remained for the strange little Uranian scientist, Moko, a life-long enemy of totalitarianism, to carve the epitaph.

Succinctly, he said:

"One less dictatorship."

CHAPTER SEVEN
Trouble on Tela

THEY came at last to Suorz, and asked at the Dau colony whether Znz and his Lundar cruiser had returned there.

The answer was in the negative.

"Where could that devil have gone to?" Wolf demanded savagely, pacing the floor of his cabin aboard the *Ghost*. "No one can vanish completely. Not even out in the void."

"Chief," interrupted Ivar hesitantly, "ain't there one chance you ain't thought of?"

"Such as?"

"Ra, Chief."

Across the room, Orcutt shuddered. Wolf glared at his mate.

"It's a physical impossibility," he snapped. "Even if he'd wanted to, and tried to, Znz couldn't have gotten his vessel to a point where it could have been hit. If I'd thought he could, with Meersa on board as she was, I'd have never considered the idea."

Moko chimed in: "I agree. I checked that course. Not a chance of Znz hitting or being hit." A pause. "Lots of asteroids around, anyhow. Znz could be there. Might have stopped off anywhere."

"But what are we going to do?" demanded Orcutt, licking his pale lips in worried fashion. "We cannot search every asteroid. It would take forever—"

"We won't have to." Wolf was suddenly decisive. "In all this talk about Znz hiding on an asteroid, we're all forgetting that the average asteroid is a pretty barren spot, incapable of supporting life."

"You mean that we should search only some of the asteroids—?"

"No. It would be a waste of time to search any of them. Stop and consider: if you were Znz, what would you do?"

Ivar snorted. "Huh! That's easy. Blow my head off with a ray gun before you catched up to me, that's what I'd do. And so would anyone else with a brain above an amoeba."

"Hmmm..." Moko considered. "With Ra and Virna both destroyed, 's not much left. Just Tela and Suorz. Not on Suorz, either. That leaves Tela..."

"It could not be Tela," Orcutt moped tonelessly. "Znz and Rsk now are deadly enemies because of Znz' revolt. Znz could not go there—"

"But emergencies make strange bedfellows," cut in Wolf grimly. "Anyhow, I'm wondering if the destruction of Virna wouldn't be just enough to bring those two cutthroats together again."

THE young Dau still shook his head. "It is too much to believe," he said. "Besides, if Meersa is on Tela, and in the hands of the Lundars there, she might as well be dead. No one could help her—"

"Still and all, we're going to have a try at it."

"What—" The princess' stocky aide jerked alert.

"Yes." Wolf nodded. "Better to do something, and have it the wrong thing, than to grow old waiting but accomplishing nothing."

"But how—"

"The *Ghost's* in the best of shape. We'll try a little raiding."

A lumbering Lundar freighter of the type used before the advent of Ra's power became the buccaneers' victim. It was just leaving Tela for Suorz when they struck. Two Saturnians dragged its captain before Wolf Stone.

"Who's ruling Tela?" the pirate chief demanded, his blue eyes looking straight into the Lundar's red orbs. "Is it Rsk or Znz?"

For a moment the captive hesitated, then decided it would be best to answer.

"It is as before," he said at last in a surly tone. "Rsk is gar, Znz sub-gar. After the revolt, Rsk would have killed Znz—in fact, he went so far as to put a price on his head. But when Virna was destroyed, and Ra with it, he thought better of it and allowed Znz to return, so that you might not destroy them separately."

Wolf glanced over at Orcutt and Ivar. "See?" he cried triumphantly. "What did I tell you?"

And then, to the Lundar captain:

"What happened to the Princess Meersa? Where's she?"

The other shrugged his great shoulders. "I do not know. Who cares what happens to the women of a subject race?"

At that, Orcutt sprang forward, but Ivar—at a gesture from Wolf—held him back.

"Why waste your energy?" the spaceman said. "We have more important work to do."

The young Dau sagged back, eyes still smouldering.

"But what can we do?" he asked hopelessly. "You have worked miracles, Wolf Stone. But even you cannot hope to attack Tela with one space ship."

A thin smile lit up the Earthman's face. He motioned the Saturnians to drag the Lundar out. Then he crossed the cabin to where Orcutt had slumped down. He gripped the stocky youth's shoulder.

"Sometimes, Orcutt," he declared quietly, "a frontal attack is not the best policy."

The other did not answer.

"This is one of them," Wolf went on. "I think it's fairly reasonable to believe that Meersa is somewhere on Tela. Certainly they wouldn't kill her just for the fun of it—"

A VENUSIAN burst in. "A small space ship is coming out from Tela, my commander," he announced. "Shall we seize it?"

Wolf nodded. "Might as well. Now that the Lundars haven't got Ra's power, we can outrun them every time."

The Venusian grinned. "It will not be hard this time, my commander, for this craft has seen us, yet does not flee."

"They're not running?" Wolf frowned. "I don't like the sound of that. That smells like a trap."

Together, the little group hurried to the telescreen.

"Look at the way they are maneuvering!" cried Orcutt. "They are asking that we parley."

"Yes." Wolf turned to the navigator-pilot. "Let them come alongside. But watch out for tricks."

A few moments later, not a Lundar, but a Dau, came aboard through the *Ghost's* airlock.

"Niker!" cried Orcutt.

The other nodded. "Yes, Orcutt. It is I. Though when I consider my mission, I am ashamed to confess it."

"Your mission? What do you mean, my good friend?"

"You know that Rsk and Znz again rule Tela together?"

"Yes. Of course."

"I come as their messenger, Orcutt."

"You! Their messenger?"

Niker smiled sadly. "Yes, Orcutt. I have no choice but to do as they tell me. The lives of my wife and children hang in the balance."

"Of course. I should have known." Orcutt patted the other's shoulder in consolation. Then: "But what message do you bring, Niker?"

"Our princess, Meersa, is a prisoner, Orcutt."

"Then they *have* got her!"

"Yes—"

Anguish flooded Orcutt's face. He interrupted: "What is it they plan to do with her? Quick, Niker! Tell me!"

"Orcutt, it breaks my heart to tell you, but—they say you raiders must leave the solar system forever. If you agree, Princess Meersa will be allowed to live out her life as a prisoner. She will never be free, but she will be kindly treated and made as happy as possible."

"And if we do not leave?"

"You remember the great zoo?"

"Yes. Of course."

"And the quirsts of Suorz? The small, poisonous snakes with arms?"

"Yes."

"If you do not leave, Orcutt, Meersa will be thrown into their cage at the zoo. She will die the awful, lingering death their fangs bring."

"No! It can't be! Not even the Lundars would do a thing so horrible—"

"It is what they threaten, Orcutt.

They give you but twenty-four hours to decide. At the end of that time I am to be returned with your sworn promise to leave, and with that of Wolf Stone. And by the time my little ship reaches the great central port, this vessel, the *Ghost*, must already be on its way out into the void, leaving this solar system forever."

THE shoulders of Orcutt the Dau slumped hopelessly. His broad face was suddenly haggard. When he spoke, it was in the low stumbling monotone of a broken man.

"There is no need to wait twenty-four hours for our answer," he said. "There can be but one decision. We shall leave, Niker. Now. Meersa—"

"No!"

The savage intensity of Wolf Stone's voice brought both Daus up short. They spun to face the raider chief.

All through their discussion, he had leaned silently against the cabin wall. Now he stood clear, feet wide apart, back stiff and unbending, head thrust forward just a trifle with the very fierceness of his emotion. His thumbs were thrust into the broad *yako*-leather belt that girded his waist. Coal-black hair awry, blue eyes chill with menace against the bronzed background of his lean hard face, he looked his name—savage and dangerous and cunning as a gaunt old timber wolf; hard and unyielding as the very rock of ages.

"No!" he repeated. "We don't leave, now or ever, until we're ready to go."

"But Meersa—" choked Orcutt.

The Earthman turned on him with all the ferocity of a wounded tiger.

"Do you think Wolf Stone's promise means nothing?"

"Your promise?"

"The day that Meersa saved my life, I swore to her that I'd see her enemies in hell. The least I can do is to die trying to put them there."

"But Meersa!" the young Dau whispered again. "Do you not see, Wolf? Were we to attack, she would die a death worse than any you can imagine. We cannot risk it—"

"Do you know this Niker well? Do you trust him?"

Orcutt nodded. "With my life," he said simply. "He is one of my oldest friends. And of Meersa's."

Wolf turned on Niker.

"Do you know that the Lundars have the princess a prisoner?" he demanded.

"I have seen her. I have talked with her."

"All right, then. Come on, Orcutt. We've got to work fast."

"But what can we do—"

"We've got twenty-four hours, haven't we? Empires have fallen in less than that."

Orcutt remained unconvinced. "We cannot attack Tela," he said. "The sheer force of numbers would overwhelm even your crew, Wolf."

"If we attacked openly. Which we shan't do."

"What do you mean?"

"There are times for force, and there are times for strategy. This, I think, is a time for strategy."

ORCUTT shook his head in bewilderment. "I do not understand," he confessed.

"It's pretty obvious, isn't it, that we can't just dive the *Ghost* down on Tela?"

"Yes."

"So we have to figure out another way of fighting. Something that the Lundars can't imagine happening." A pause. "What do you figure they'd least expect, Orcutt?"

The young Dau frowned then shook his head. "There is nothing we could do that they would not be prepared for, Wolf Stone," he said at last.

A tight grin passed over the Earthman's face.

"I think there is, Orcutt," he declared. "I think there is something so utterly absurd that no Lundar would dream of it happening."

"What is it?"

Again the raider chief grinned.

"I, personally, am going to invade Tela," he announced.

"You mean—"

"I mean that instead of trying to attack the planet openly, I'm going to sneak down in a torpedo ship. I'm going to prowl around a bit and see if I can't dope out a way to get Meersa away from the Lundars. After that we can work on the problem of breaking their control over the planet."

Stark amazement, then new hope, leaped into Orcutt's eyes.

"I shall come with you!" he cried excitedly.

"It would seem like a good idea. You know your way around Tela, and I don't. It would help a lot to have you around."

"Me, too, chief." grunted Ivar from the background.

Wolf shook his head. "Sorry, Ivar. No dice."

"Huh?" The big Jupiterian peered at the buccaneer leader as if unable to believe his ears. "I don't get it, chief. You ain't got no idea of leaving me here, have you?"

"I'm afraid so, Ivar."

"But—"

"It's got to be that way. In the first place, the torpedo ships carry only two people. In the second, we need someone competent to stay in command of the *Ghost*. Third, there's no disguise in the universe that could make you pass as someone who belonged on Tela; because neither Daus, Lundars, nor Bans have four arms and one eye."

"You'll need help, though, chief. You got to have—"

"If two can't do the job, neither can three, Ivar. No, I'm afraid you'll have to let Orcutt and me handle this assignment."

Orcutt interrupted: "When do we leave?"

"Just as soon as we can get ready. Which should take about fifteen minutes. We've got to work fast."

SOMETHING besides night fell on Tela that evening. For with the dusk, the slim, sinister form of a torpedo ship settled silently to the planet's surface, on that edge of the badlands lying closest to the great capitol city.

"The first thing we must do is to procure Dau clothing for ourselves, and cosmetics with which to whiten your skin." Orcutt explained to Wolf as they climbed out of their tiny craft. "Only then will it be safe to begin our search."

"Right," agreed the Earthman. "Well, let's get going."

"It will be difficult," his companion confessed. "I do not know quite how we can obtain garments."

Wolf grinned. "Where can we find a Dau or two?" he asked. "I'll demonstrate for you."

They had been walking as they talked. Now they found themselves entering the outermost suburb. Ahead of them a Dau hurried toward a ramshackle hovel.

"There's a Dau now!" exclaimed the Earthman.

"Oh, my poor people!" choked Orcutt. He jerked his head toward the shanties, "See how the Lundars force them to live!"

"Come on." snapped Wolf, breaking into a swift, silent run, "This isn't any time to talk sociology. We've got too much to do."

"What…" Orcutt began.

"Shhh!"

On they sped. Then the Dau on the street ahead caught the whisper of their footsteps. He started to turn.

Wolf launched himself through the air like a veritable human projectile. His shoulder crashed into the Dau's legs below the knee in a perfect tackle. The man went down, his shocked cry still sticking in his throat. The next instant the Earthman's fist drove home on the Dau's jaw with a meaty *thunk!*

"O.K.," Wolf clipped. "Get 'em off him. Hurry up!"

"But he is of my people! We cannot rob—"

"Do you think this is a good time for a shopping expedition? We've got work to do. Hurry up!"

Orcutt hastily obeyed, while the Dau whom Wolf had downed groaningly stirred in his coma. A moment later the two adventurers were gone, leaving a shivering, swearing, half-stunned—and definitely naked—victim behind them.

A few minutes later they repeated the process, then held up a shop handling cosmetics to obtain some of the thick, white cream used by Dau women to cover complexion blemishes.

Wolf smeared it on in a nearby alley.

"Now," he announced grimly, "we're ready to start work in earnest. Where's Meersa likely to be?"

His companion meditated for a moment.

"Now that Ra has been destroyed, I do not believe she would be held in the prison we were in formerly," he said finally. "Instead, they probably would have placed her in one of the jails reserved for minor offenders." A pause. "But then they may be keeping her in the Lundar headquarters, or some similar place."

"Is there any way you can find out definitely?"

"No. I know of none. I asked Niker—who certainly should have known, more than anyone else—and he told me that her hiding place was being kept a secret by the Lundars to discourage any rescue attempt by our people." The young Dau's face grew gloomy again. "You see we have little chance. The Lundars have done their work well. They are taking no chances on escape this time."

FOR a long moment Wolf Stone stood silent. Then:

"What jail would they probably have her in if they were keeping her in one?"

"The central one. It is in the great Tribunal Hall, where you were brought before Rsk."

"Good." A pause. "What do Daus get put in jail for? Small offenses, that is."

Looking somewhat puzzled, Orcutt answered: "The most common offense is drunkenness. All too many of my people have a taste for *apolosa.*"

"Where can we get some?"

"At any store."

"Then come on. Let's buy some."

"Wait." Orcutt held the Earthman back. "What is it you plan?"

Wolf grinned. "Apparently the only way to find Meersa is to get thrown in jail ourselves. Yet we don't want to be pinched on a serious charge, because that would bring too much investigation and questioning. So I figured a nice, noisy apolosa drunk would do the job."

"But after we are in, we cannot get out!" the stocky Dau protested. "We should have to throw our ray guns away or they would be found when we were searched—"

"Uh-uh." Wolf shook his head. "In the first place, I've been in jail on many a planet, and I've never seen one where a drunk gets searched very thoroughly. Besides, we're going to hide our guns like this—" Raising the flowing, robe-like Dau garment which he wore, he strapped his heavy pistol high between his legs. "That'll pass anything but a complete strip," he explained. "Fix yours the same way."

An hour later the pair was lurching solemnly along the street on which the Tribunal Hall fronted. Wolf carried a big apolosa bottle in his hand.

"Remember, you do the talking," he hissed in last-minute instruction. "My accent isn't any too hot."

Orcutt, the Dau, nodded.

The next instant they came abreast the two giant Lundars who guarded the entrance to the building.

Wolf reared back and stared up at them, beautifully and belligerently drunk. He was a sight to behold. Mud smeared his face and his clothes. Saliva I trickled from the corners of his loosely held lips, to join streams on his chin and thence drip to the ground. A strong aura of apolosa hung about him.

"Go on, now!" one of the guards growled. "Get moving, you drunken scum."

Very deliberately the disguised Earthman spat squarely between the Lundar's feet.

"Why, you—!" The guard started forward, his red eyes glaring.

"You le' my frien' 'lone!" burbled Orcutt soddenley.

The other guard intervened.

"They're drunk," he soothed his comrade. "They don't know what they're doing."

"Well,"—the first guard hesitated, caught between two fires—"well, I ought to throw them in Drunken Daus! They're worse riff-raff than the Bans."

"Who you 'sultin'?" screamed Orcutt angrily.

"Yeah!" roared Wolf. He hurled his empty apolosa bottle at the head of the guard who had tried to act as peacemaker.

The guard ducked. "Why, you scum!" he yelped, as the container whistled past his ear. "You want trouble, do you? Well, you'll get it! We'll see how you like spending a few days in jail!"

Suiting his actions to his word, he sprang forward, caught Wolf firmly by the collar and dragged him into the hall. His partner, hauling Orcutt, came close at his heels.

CHAPTER EIGHT
Quirsts Must Eat

AS WOLF had predicted, the search made of the prisoners was definitely on the superficial side. A burly Lundar sergeant heard the guards' complaints, then promptly consigned the Earthman and his companion to a week in jail. Turned over to another guard, the two were herded down a long corridor toward Tela's equivalent of a drunk tank.

"That door," Orcutt whispered as the Lundar hurried them along the passageway. He nodded to indicate an impressively solid panel set in the right-hand wall of the hall. "If Meersa's here, she will be on the level to which it leads."

The other gave a great sigh. His legs buckled under him. His muscles no longer functioned. He sprawled on the floor, a sodden heap.

Lipping an oath, the Lundar bent down to pull the disguised Earthman erect. But his hand never touched the prisoner's shoulder.

Instead, Wolf rolled over. His ray gun was in his hand, his eyes suddenly very cold and blue and sober. He thrust the weapon's muzzle against the guard's chest.

"There's a door we want opened," he snapped. "Get moving, if you want to live!"

Close beside him, Orcutt—his gun also now drawn—forced the Lundar back. Together, the two adventurers pressed toward the door.

It was locked.

"Blast it!" Wolf commanded.

Orcutt triggered his ray-gun at the lock, while the buccaneer chief continued to keep the guard covered.

"Wolf! It's broken!"

For the barest fraction of a second, the Earthman's eyes flashed to Orcutt and the now-open door.

"Look out!"

The panic in the stocky Dau's voice sent Wolf swiveling back to the guard like an animated gun turret, every muscle tense, every nerve on edge.

The Lundar had taken advantage of that momentary break in the raider's attention. He was lunging forward, great arms swinging. His red eyes were like pools of blood.

"Stop! You fool!"

On the Lundar came. His ten-inch fingers clutched hungrily for the space pirate's throat.

The Earthman dropped to one knee. His lean face was grim. His finger tightened on the ray gun's trigger.

The Lundar stopped in mid-strike. His face contorted with sudden shock and pain. The breath went out of him in a rush. He pitched forward, onto his face. Wolf jumped aside barely in time to avoid the monster's falling body.

"Wolf! Did he hurt you?"

The raider chief shook his head.

"No," he answered, "but he's messed things up. Now we'll have to work fast."

"What do you mean?"

"Isn't it pretty obvious? If we could have kept him alive, we could have made him go with us. As it is, the minute his body's discovered, the hunt for us will be on."

"YES. I see. What shall we do with him?"

Wolf glanced about. Then:

"There's no place in this corridor to hide him. The only thing we can do is to drag him through this door you just opened. Then we'll shut it and pray that no one has cause to use it. Hurry!"

Together, the pair somehow hauled the Lundar's corpse through the doorway. The portal was at the foot of a stairway. To get the unbelievably heavy body far enough up the steps so that they could close the door at first seemed an impossibility. But at last, straining and tugging, they managed to drag the dead guard inside.

"All right. That's done. Now we've got to rush!"

They sprinted up the stairs. Blasted open another door, at the head, and hurried down a corridor similar to the one below.

"The more important prisoners are on this level," Orcutt explained between gasps as they ran onward. "If Princess Meersa is in the central jail, this is where she should be."

Another door loomed, solid save for a small grated opening near its top.

The young Dau caught Wolf's arm.

"Beyond are cells," he whispered. "In the center corridor a guard is usually stationed."

Wolf glanced up at the portal. Like all the others it was solidly built, and on such a scale as to permit its use by the twelve-foot Lundars.

"That's bad," he clipped. "By the time we could smash that lock with our ray-guns, the guard inside would be ready to give us a warm reception."

"If he were alive, no doubt he would," Orcutt retorted grimly. "Give me a leg up, Wolf Stone."

The other eyed him. "You mean to kill him?" he asked.

Orcutt nodded. "Yes. I do not like killing. Not even of Lundars. But when my princess is in danger, it becomes necessary." And then, his face strained: "Come! Help me up! We must hurry."

Wolf lifted him until he could sight his ray gun through the grating. Grimly the young Dau brought the weapon level; squeezed the trigger.

The thud of his feet as he jumped down was echoed by the dull thump of a heavy body falling. A moment later the pair had blasted the lock loose. They hurried into the cellblock.

In the center of the floor lay the crumpled form of a dead Lundar guard, while from both sides of the room Daus stared out of their cramped cells at the newcomers. They greeted Orcutt with a chorus of low, joyful cries.

He silenced them with a gesture.

"Where is the Princess Meersa?" he demanded.

FOR a long moment silence hung heavy over the imprisoned natives of Tela. But at last one wrinkled aged Dau broke the tension.

"She is…in the tower, Orcutt," he reported in a tone of mourning.

"In the tower!"

The others hung their heads in silent confirmation.

Orcutt's face was terrible to see.

"They have put her in the tower, Wolf!" he cried, as if the other had not heard.

"I got that. But I don't understand what it means. What is the tower?"

"No. You would not know." The stocky Dau licked his lips feverishly. "You see, Wolf Stone, the Lundar gars must be amused...amused by the women of Tela!"

"What?" The Earthman's face showed incredulity. "That doesn't seem possible, Orcutt. After all, the Lundars are twelve feet tall—"

"No, no. You do not understand. The Lundars are not as we; they are themselves sexless. But it pleases them to give Dau girls to the males of other races—the Ban primitives of Suorz, the Ios of the far asteroids. The horror, the struggles, of our women amuse them, then—"

"The damned degenerated, sadistic *gratchs!*" grated Wolf. "I've seen every corner of two solar systems, but never have I heard the like of that!"

He turned on the wrinkled Dau who had told them Meersa was in the tower.

"When did they take her?"

"Only this evening, I believe," came the answer. "Our guard taunted us with it when he came on duty."

Wolf's eyes flashed. "Then there's a good chance we can reach her before...anything happens," he snapped. Then, to Orcutt: "How do we get to the tower?"

"There is a lift—what you call an elevator."

"Then let's go."

"Do not leave us!" cried one of the Daus. "Free us first."

Already moving, the Earthman paused. He tossed his ray gun to the man who had spoken.

"You can burn your way out with this," he clipped. "Don't try to follow us. It's every man for himself now."

Then he and Orcutt were running full-tilt down another corridor.

"The lift is close by here," the young Dau panted. "We must be careful. It is well-guarded."

They rounded a corner—and ran straight into three Lundar guards grouped about the entrance to the monster elevator.

Wolf—unarmed now—hurled himself at the first of the ogrish creatures. The Lundar was standing with his back to the Earthman. Wolf's shoulder crashed into the back of the giant's knees.

The guard sprawled, his legs knocked from under him. His body toppled in front of the second Lundar, now turning to face the attack; sent him, too, staggering. The pair collapsed to the floor in a threshing tangle of huge arms and legs.

But the third giant jumped free. His great red eyes flared as he took in the situation. His hand flashed toward the light gun at his hip.

ORCUTT—spraddle-legged, his stocky body twisted sidewise as he braked himself to a sliding halt—already was bringing up his ray gun. He triggered a spray of death square into the Lundar's face. Watched the giant's jaw sag, his body crumple.

But even as he saw the first enemy go down, he was spinning to face the menace of the other two Lundars.

Wolf was rolling free of the struggling pair on the floor. Somehow, in the chaos, his fingers had clutched a Lundar light gun. Already he was blasting the purple bolts into them.

One of the creatures went limp. The other tried to tear free.

Orcutt's ray gun nailed him through the throat before he could so much as get his feet under him.

Wolf staggered erect. He thrust the light gun he had used into his belt, then fumbled for another among the corpses.

"That was close!" he said. The light of reckless battle was shining in his eyes.

Orcutt nodded. "Yes. But what now?"

"The elevator—can we get it?"

"Yes. These buttons—" The Dau indicated a panel of vari-colored buzzers.

"Get one."

The Dau moved to obey. But before he could reach the panel, the great doors swung back. A Lundar operator gaped out at them.

Wolf and Orcutt fired as one. The giant in the car slammed back against the rear wall, dead before he hit it.

"The Lundars must have rung for him before we came." breathed Orcutt.

"Yes. Come on." Wolf stepped into the car.

"But what about the bodies?"

"Bodies!" Wolf snarled the word as if it were a curse. "Bodies! Bodies! More bodies! Yes, we'll have to take care of 'em. We've got to stall off pursuit as long as possible."

"Could we perhaps place all of them in the elevator?"

"No. That wouldn't help any." The Earthman stood tense, eyes probing every niche and cranny of the corridor. Then: "Will the elevator work with the doors open?"

"Perhaps. We could try."

A few seconds of frantic experiment revealed that they could hold the car's doors open, yet still raise it a couple of feet above floor level.

"Down the shaft with 'em." grated the raider chief. "They won't find 'em there for hours."

In less than a minute, the corpses of the Lundars were hurtling into the depths.

Scrambling into the car and closing the doors, Wolf and Orcutt sped upward. At last a flashing light indicated that they had reached the top floor.

"There will be guards here." warned the young Dau as he gripped the door lever. "We must be ready."

Wolf whipped out the two light guns he had taken from the dead giants. His lean face was hard, his chill eyes filled with menace.

"Let's go!" he clipped.

THE doors swung open. Two guards spun to face the raiders.

The Earthman's guns belched purple light. The Lundars died.

Together, Wolf and Orcutt sprang from the elevator, half-expecting more trouble from some new angle. But they found no signs of life.

"This is the tower," explained the Dau. "Somewhere on this level we should find Meersa, if she remains alive."

They hurried through one empty room after another. Then, just as the awful qualms of defeat were rising in their hearts, they came upon a locked door.

"Maybe this is it!" Wolf cried.

"None of the others have been locked, if that means anything."

They blasted at the lock. Hurled themselves against the stubborn portal.

Suddenly, then, it gave. They plunged into the room beyond.

There, huddled in a sobbing heap on a great divan, lay the one they sought.

"Meersa!" cried Orcutt, springing to her side. He dropped to his knees beside the couch. "My darling, what have they done to you?"

The girl raised her tear-stained face. She stared at her aide. Then at the grim, silent figure of Wolf Stone, still standing in the doorway. Incredulity and joy mingled in her expression. She tried to speak, but her voice betrayed her. Laughing and sobbing at once, her arms sought the young Dau. But even as she clung to him, she gestured the Earthman closer also.

"Oh, my friends!" she gasped at last. "I had given up all hope. Until this evening, when the Lundars brought me here to the tower, I kept telling myself that somehow I would be saved. That you would find a way to rescue me.

"Then, quite early, the guards came and dragged me from my cell. They told me that it pleased Rsk to break my pride by giving me to an Io—an awful, slavering beast without a mind; a creature knowing naught but instinctive lust—"

"But they did not do it, Meersa. Tell me they did not do it," begged Orcutt.

The girl's hand caressed his shoulder. She smiled, a wistful tender smile.

"No, my faithful one, they did not do it," she reassured him. "Rsk must be busy, for they have not yet come for me."

She turned to the Earthman. Took his hands in hers.

"Forgive me, Wolf Stone, for doubting you," she begged, adoration shining in her eyes. "Never have I known a man like unto you. In our whole solar system there has never been such a one—"

The hint of a smile touched the adventurer's thin lips. The icy blue eyes softened just a little.

"I pledged my word I'd fight for you and protect you," he said, "and Wolf Stone's word is never broken."

Then:

"But this isn't the time to talk. We're not out of this mess yet—"

"I know." But Meersa's eyes were still on his, her hands still holding him. "I can hardly believe it," she whispered. "That two men could somehow fight their way to me—"

"Come on!" Wolf interrupted. "I'm sorry, Princess, but we've got to hurry."

And then from the doorway behind them, came a voice as cold and deadly as the clang of hell's own doors:

"No, do not hurry. First you must taste my hospitality!"

It was the voice of Rsk, gar of all the Lundars!

EVEN as he whirled, Wolf's hands flashed toward the guns hanging heavy in his belt. But he had forgotten that Meersa still clung to him. Her grip slowed him the fraction of a second in his draw.

Perhaps it was as well; had his guns come up he would have died where he stood. For Rsk stood squarely in the middle of the big doorway, and flanking him on either side was a Lundar guard with drawn light-gun.

Now they moved forward, and one of the guards relieved Wolf and Orcutt of their weapons, while the second kept the raiders and Meersa covered.

Another Lundar followed Rsk into the room. It was Znz, his pale, sinister face alight with evil joy.

"You should not have helped the Daus below to escape, Wolf Stone." he gloated. "Like the clumsy fools they are, they stumbled into the hands of our guards before they had even gotten off their own levels. We knew without asking, then, where we could find you. Eh, Rsk?"

But the giant gar's original words apparently had exhausted his self-control. Now he was almost trembling with rage. His voice quavered with fury.

"You *chitzas!*" he raved. "You *starbos!* Once I said I'd make you pray for death. And now I will! The three of you together, I'll watch you die. Oh, what agonies you'll suffer—"

His hate was awful to behold. Meersa, her eyes wide with undisguised terror, clung to Orcutt. The young Dau, in turn, held her close to him. But his own face was taut with strain and he licked his dry lips nervously with the tip of his tongue.

Not Wolf Stone.

Contemptuously the raider chief eyed the Lundar gar and sub-gar from head to toe. Not a sign of fear crept into the blue diamond chips that were his eyes. No tremor of panic racked his lean frame. He stood before them, reckless and defiant, with his thumbs hooked into the broad belt that girded in his flowing robe-like Dau garment, and a mocking, daredevil's smile twisting his mouth.

"You'll die a separate death for every Lundar who perished on Virna." raged Rsk. "Yes, and on Ra, too!" A pause. Then: "Well, you *chitza*, do you fear to speak? Is your throat too dry with terror to give out words?"

Wolf laughed in his face.

"Do I look afraid?" he demanded with a sneer that sent the gar into new spasms of fury. "Do I look like the kind of a cowardly dog who'd crawl on his knees to you for mercy? So why should I give you the satisfaction of answering you?

"But one thing I'll tell you, Rsk. One piece of advice I'll give you: kill us now, while you've got the chance, if you want to live yourself.

"Once before you swore you'd kill me, but I got away. I wiped out two of your planets, and I set your puny, puling empire rocking on its heels.

"Give me another chance, and I'll knock it down around your ears like a glass house in an earthquake. I'll quit bothering with subordinates, and concentrate on killing you, yourself, Rsk, and that crawling traitor, Znz, that stands behind you—"

"I'll give you your chance to die!" screamed Rsk. "Right now, I'll give you your chance." And, to the guards: "Take him below! Take them all! To the zoo with them!"

Watchful and deadly, the guards herded the captives out of the room. Across the anteroom into the elevator.

TWENTY levels lower, they left the car again. Went down a corridor. Through the Tribunal Hall's vast museum wing. Past exhibits ranging from specimens of primitive Ban beadwork, to a huge, carefully insulated chunk of radioactive ore from the pits of Ra, to the delicate, beautiful products of skilled Dau metal workers.

And, at last, out of the museum and into the zoo, where the Lundars had gathered specimens of the wild life of every planet, every asteroid, in this entire solar system—*peens*, hideous, pterodactyl-like, with monstrous, bony wings; *gratchs*, blind, burrowing, mole-like; *yakos, stongs, jeors*...

But still the party continued. Past, one cage after another. Until finally they reached a section where a strange stench assailed their nostrils. And there they stopped.

"Quirsts," choked Meersa in a voice that trembled with loathing.

"Quirsts!" echoed the gloating tones of Rsk.

The group was standing behind a railing. Ten feet beyond it were the bars of a cage. Straining his eyes, Wolf peered at the creatures within the den. When he saw them, his stomach nearly rose in revolt.

Nowhere in the length and breadth of two solar systems, had he seen the like. Hideous with warts and scales, these snake-like things had *arms!* Tiny, perfectly developed, almost human arms! They darted about their cage like flashes of light, glaring malevolently out at the intruders with beady reptilian eyes. Like every other creature in this strange solar system, their color was a fish-belly white, result of the sun's deficiency in various rays.

The Earthman fought down the nausea that swirled within him. When he spoke, his voice was steady.

"So these are quirsts!" he remarked interestedly. And, to the Lundars: "Just how are our fates linked with theirs?"

It was Znz who answered. His tone surged with triumph.

"Even quirsts must eat!" he said.

CHAPTER NINE
Pirate Payoff

"THE quirst is poisonous," the sub-gar went on, gloatingly. "So poisonous that even their breaths can sometimes bring death. They will strike at any living thing, and without provocation. Paralysis is immediate, but death—a death in agony, I might add—is slow in coming. When you and your Dau friends are placed inside that cage, Wolf Stone"—he rubbed his hands together with unholy glee—"these creatures will swarm over you, clutching you, biting you, gnawing at you. They are hungry, Wolf Stone—"

"I've been bitten by snakes before," the Earthman retorted caustically, "but none as slimy as you, Znz. Now I'll have a chance to see if these quirsts you're so proud of can match you."

The sub-gar tensed at the jibe.

"You'll sing a different song when you face the quirsts!" he snarled. "You and this Orcutt and the tender Princess Meersa you're so fond of—"

"No!" cried Orcutt aloud. His whole body was shaking. "No! Not Meersa! Do what you want with us, Znz, but free Meersa—"

"Shut up!" slashed Wolf. "Would you crawl in front of these gorillas for any cause? We'll go, and we'll go together, and to hell with them, one and all!"

He vaulted the low rail that held visitors a safe distance from the cages. Meersa climbed after him, her lovely pale face as proudly defiant as his own. Orcutt brought up the rear.

"Good girl!" the raider chief muttered in Meersa's ear as he helped her over. And, to Orcutt: "On your toes! The cards aren't all down yet!"

Now one of the guards came forward. He had donned a strange garment resembling a flying suit. Moving up to the door of the cage, he grasped the lever.

"Come on!" he growled.

Never had Wolf Stone appeared more swaggering and defiant than at that moment. But there was a cold sheen of sweat over his forehead, and his mouth felt parched and cottony.

He approached the cage. Not a detail missed his cold-eyed scrutiny, and every impression was torn to frantic shreds by the fine mechanism of his brain as he searched past and present and future, and the whole universe, for even the slightest hope.

The quirsts, he noted, were only eight inches long, but they moved with a speed and deadliness that made the cobra's strike seem lackadaisical. The bars of their cage were covered with mesh netting in fine testimony to the creatures' dangerous character, while the door had a two-foot-high sill beneath it— complete with down-slanting guard spikes on the inside—to prevent their climbing out, even should the door itself accidentally be left open.

A sudden light gleamed in the adventurer's eyes. He bared his teeth in a savage grin.

"Why do you move so slowly, Wolf Stone?" jibed Znz.

"Yes!" taunted Rsk. "What's wrong, brave man? Get into the cage and die!"

The Lundar in the strange suit swung open the door of bars.

Wolf clenched his teeth. He could feel a rill of icy sweat go trickling down his back. Drawing a deep breath, breathing a silent prayer, he stepped toward the open door—and carefully stumbled over his own feet.

IT WAS well done. Rsk and Znz howled with ghoulish laughter. And Wolf careened violently into Meersa and Orcutt. The force of his blow shoved them sideways, toward the hinge side of the cage door.

Now he was ready. Now the stage was set. Wolf could feel the blood drain from his face. But he strode forward.

Then, so suddenly it was hard to follow, he struck.

Like lightning, he sprang behind the Lundar. His shoulder crashed into the giant's hip. At the same instant, his foot came down in front of those of the guard.

An ancient trick. But always a good one. The Lundar tripped. Pitched forward. Plunged headlong—under the directive and impetus of the raider's heave—over the doorsill and into the quirsts' cage.

Even as the Lundar toppled, Wolf sprang clear. In one wild leap he was across the falling giant's body. His arm caught Meersa and Orcutt. Slammed them back against the cage, close beside the door's hinges. Simultaneously he caught the locking lever. Swung the door wide open and on back, against the three of them, like a protective shield against the quirsts.

From beginning to end, the maneuver had taken less than three seconds. Seconds while Rsk and Znz and the second guard stood paralyzed with disbelief and shock.

But now, suddenly, they realized what the buccaneer chief had done—

Across the prone body of the fallen Lundar, sprawled over the doorsill, half in the cage and half out, the quirsts were leaping!

Over the human bridge they came, out of the cage and into the aisleway. Swarming, scurrying, squirming, in a torrent of sudden death.

Shrieking in panic, Rsk, Znz, and the guard fled, their prisoners forgotten. But not far. Nothing alive could outdistance those hideous, awful creatures that came after, tiny arms outstretched, in an insatiable kill-lust.

Gar, sub-gar, and guard—they went down almost together, the little Suorzian monsters nipping and clawing at their heels and legs. In less than half a minute their great bodies were mottled with the creatures.

Meersa buried her horror-distraught face against Orcutt's broad shoulder.

"Into the cage!" snapped Wolf. "It's empty now, but those devils will be back for us in a few seconds."

They clambered inside, the Earthman pausing barely long enough to snatch the light gun from the stunned Lundar whose body still lay sprawled across the doorsill.

"Now help me dump him outside," Wolf ordered. "His suit apparently protects him from the quirsts' bites."

A moment later, that job done, they swung the door closed.

And barely in time, too.

THE quirsts were coming back. Like foul figments of an evil imagination, they gathered around the cage, their beady little eyes gleaming with blood lust.

Even Wolf Stone shuddered.

"Here's hoping that story about even their breaths being poisonous is just superstition," he remarked.

Orcutt, staring out at the creatures in horrid fascination, nodded shakily and held Meersa the tighter.

"Yes," he agreed. "I, too, pray you are right." A pause. "But now, Wolf, how do we escape?"

"Have we but escaped one menace to be trapped by another?" echoed Meersa. "We cannot leave, or we will meet the fate of those...out there." Her eyes indicated the lumps of lifeless flesh that had been the Lundars.

"No." Wolf shook his head. He raised the light gun he had taken from the guard. "We'll see how those devils like a spray of this."

He triggered the weapon. Purple light washed between the bars of the cage. Broke over the quirsts in a wave of death. They dropped like flies. Yet such was their strange mentality that the survivors of that first blast, instead of fleeing, rushed close to nuzzle obscenely at their fallen fellows. Within three minutes, the last lay dead.

The Earthman swung open the cage door.

"We're free!" he cried. "Lundars and quirsts alike, we've beaten them!"

"I can hardly believe it!" whispered Princess Meersa. "I feel as if it were all a dream—half nightmare, half glorious vision."

"I know," agreed the raider chief. He walked over to where the corpses of Rsk and Znz and the guard lay, stared down at them for a moment in silence. Then:

"Look at them—Rsk and Znz, gar and sub-gar of all the Lundars! An hour ago they were the most powerful pair in the whole universe, from the sun to the farthest asteroid. Intelligent. Strong. Honored by their own people. Feared by all others.

"But now they're dead. Gone down before a herd of stinking slavering quirsts—crawling creatures, physically weak, practically without brains. Yet against them, Lundar power and intelligence didn't count."

The Earthman paused, shook his head slowly. His eyes were somber.

"If I were a philosopher, I might draw some kind of a truth from that—"

"Wolf! The guard!"

It was Orcutt's voice. The raider chief stopped in mid-breath. He whirled.

The other Lundar guard, the one in the protective suit whom Wolf had shoved through the cage door, was on his feet once more. On his feet and moving—running full-tilt for the zoo door that led into the museum.

LIKE a flash, the buccaneer was lunging in pursuit. But his legs could not match the twelve-foot giant's strides. By the time the Earthman had reached the entryway, the Lundar already was sprinting out the other side of the museum, far out of range of light gunfire.

Orcutt and Meersa ran up behind Wolf. The raider turned on them.

"He'll be back!" he snapped. "He, and every Lundar in the place with him."

"We must flee to the central port!" Orcutt exclaimed. "There we can seize some kind of space ship and escape to the *Ghost*."

"No."

"What? You do not want to escape, Wolf Stone?"

The space pirate's lean face was hard. "I want to get away as much as anyone," he snapped grimly, "but I want to be sure we've accomplished something, too. And if we leave now, the Lundars will still be in control on Tela. We've got to break their power."

"Yes. Of course. But how?"

There was a long moment of silence while Wolf restlessly paced the floor, his blue eyes worried beneath their chill. Then suddenly a grim smile sprang to his lips.

"The Tribunal Hall is the Lundar headquarters on Tela, right?"

Orcutt nodded. "Yes."

"Then if we could destroy the Hall, and all the Lundars in it, their control would be pretty well shot?"

This time Meersa answered.

"You are right, Wolf Stone," she said, at the same time glancing nervously toward the museum door through which guards might at any moment come charging.

"Come on, then. We've got work to do." And, to Orcutt: "Bar that door. We're going to need a couple of minutes to work this."

While the two Daus watched in baffled wonderment, the Earthman worked frantically. Switching off the lights—now, since Ra's destruction, electric-powered—he stripped wires bare.

There was a thundering at the door. Roars of a hundred Lundar guardsmen.

"Hold them, Orcutt!" shouted the buccaneer. "Give me another minute!"

The stocky Dau sprang to obey. He blasted at the giants through crevices with a light gun. For the moment forced them back.

Working like mad, Wolf now attacked the insulation surrounding the great chunk of radioactive ore from Ra, which formed one of the museum's central displays. He tore and blasted it away. Lashed a dozen of the light wires about the rock.

The Lundars again were smashing at the portal.

WOLF lunged across the hall. He ripped a long strip of cloth from his own clothing. Used it to connect the door at which the giants were battering with the light switch in such a way that the opening of the panel would turn on the power. He finished the job with a jerk. Then spun about.

"This way!" he gasped, panting with exertion. "Hurry! We can't lose a second!"

Away he dashed, running at top speed for the entrance to the zoo. Meersa and Orcutt were close on his heels.

Into the zoo they sprinted. Down its long central aisle.

Half a dozen Lundars loomed before them.

"A patrol…" gasped Orcutt. "They must have come in the back way!"

His words were drowned in Wolf Stone's snarl. Already the Earthman's light gun was blazing. The first two of the giants went down before its blast.

Then Orcutt and Meersa, too, were firing. Two more Lundars died. The remaining pair fled madly for the exit, Wolf and the young Daus in hot pursuit.

They were out of the Tribunal Hall, now. Sprinting for the entrance to the great central port a few hundred yards away. Other Lundars rose to oppose them—and died or fled.

The trio raced up stairways. Down runways.

"That space ship!" roared Wolf.

"It's the old type. It'll take off without broadcast power! Run for it!"

Panting and exhausted, they half-scrambled, half-fell aboard. Orcutt snatched at the controls. With a roar the craft hurtled down the runway. Burst out into the sky.

The next instant the little ship was rocking like a paper boat in a windstorm. It careened through space in a wild rigadoon.

Meersa, her eyes brimming with panic, clutched at the two men.

"What is it?" she cried. "What happened?"

Wolf gave her hand a steadying squeeze.

"It just means my scheme worked," he told her.

"Your scheme—?"

"Yes. You see that damned radioactive ore from Ra is wildly unstable. That's why electrolytic action always turned it into pure energy.

"I figured that if that was the case, maybe short-circuiting a lighting system through it would explode it the same way. So I fixed it so the breaking down of that door to the museum would switch on the lights. It must have worked—because the Tribunal Hall and the Lundars in it are gone!"

The girl's eyes followed the finger he pointed at the telescreen.

Where once the great building had stood, now hovered only a fog of dust and smoke.

IVAR said: "The chief? Sure, he's a swell guy. All aces."

"Yes, I know he is." Meersa sighed and tried again. "But…was he really a pirate in this other solar system from which you came? Did he kill and steal—"

The big Jupiterian grinned. "He didn't do nothing else but," he declared. "The Interplanetary Police classed him with acts of God—said they was both disasters. Why, I remember one time we was raiding Neptune—"

Again the Dau princess sighed.

"I wonder why he did it," she said softly. "To me he has been so kind and yet, a pirate…"

"Us pirates ain't so bad," defended Ivar. "We got a lot of good guys. After all, lady, there's some awful goons running our neck of the woods. Why you think Wolf turned raider in the first place?"

"Why did he?" Meersa asked eagerly, her lovely face anxious.

"It was his old man," the other explained. "He was quite a guy, too. A scientist. But some big shot in the Interplanetary Federation got down on him. Killed him and all his family. Only Wolf got away. He was just a kid, but he managed to get to the outer asteroids—the I. P. hadn't mopped up there yet, in them days.

"Well, when he growed up, he was in on a couple of revolutions. But no revolution had the chance of a space ship landing on the sun. Not with the I. P. on the job. So finally Wolf just blasted around from one planet to another, making all the trouble he could for the Federation. Believe me, lady, a lot of folks hadn't never had a square meal 'til Wolf knocked off the garrison over 'em and opened up the storehouses. There's plenty of places where they just about pray to him—"

"Ivar! You mean he was forced to be a pirate? That always he helped the oppressed as he helped us against the Lundars?"

The mate was aggrieved. "Sure. Ain't that what I been telling you all along? Wolf's a swell guy—"

"Oh, Ivar! I am so happy!"

The girl was radiant in her joy. Turning, she darted from the bewildered Jupiterian's presence. Ran down the corridor to Wolf's cabin.

The raider chief was working over a huge celestial chart. He glanced up as the princess came in. Smiling, he motioned her to a chair.

"Sit down, Meersa. Well, how's it going, now that things are on an even keel on Tela again, and you're back in the saddle?"

Meersa ignored the seat. Instead she stood before him, her lovely face just a little strained. Her fingers knotted nervously into small fists.

"Wolf Stone," she said, "I must talk to you."

Again he smiled.

"Talk ahead."

SHE swallowed hard, searched her brain for the right words. Her eyes dropped. She bit her lip. Then, in an almost embarrassed little voice:

"It is not good that a woman should rule Tela alone, Wolf."

She hesitated, but the Earthman made no move to interrupt. At last she went on.

"There should be a strong man beside me, Wolf. A man like you, to watch over my people...and over me."

Still the raider chief said nothing. There was a long moment of uncomfortable silence. At last the girl could stand it no longer. She raised her eyes. They were hurt and angry, and filled with tears. Her lower lip quivered.

"Can you not speak, Wolf Stone?" she cried. "Am I so ugly you cannot endure the thought of me? Must you make me shame myself by telling you that I want you; that I must have you; that I am asking you to marry me and rule beside me?"

The Earthman walked slowly across the cabin, then turned to face her, hands locked behind him, feet wide apart. His lean brown face was no longer hard; only weary. And the blue eyes that had been so cold and menacing now were filled with pain.

"I'm sorry, Meersa," he said, and his voice was old and tired.

"What does that mean, Wolf Stone?" she flared. "Am I not good enough—"

"Please!" He raised his hand to silence her. Ran long fingers through the jet-black of his hair. At last: "Meersa, do you realize what I am?"

The anger went out of the girl as quickly as it had come.

"I—I do not understand," she stammered.

"I'm not a king, Meersa. I'm a pirate. 'Scum of the spaceways,' the Interplanetary Police call my men and me. And they're not too far wrong—"

"But that is all past," the princess broke in passionately. "You were a pirate, yes. But it was in another world. You were forced to it. Ivar told me—"

"Forced to it?" The buccaneer leader threw her a twisted smile. "At first, maybe. But you don't play Robin Hood forever, Meersa. You get so you raid for the thrill of raiding, and for the loot, just as if you were a *Malya* from the outer asteroids—"

"But it is past!" she repeated fiercely. "Forget all that—"

"It isn't past. It can never be past."

"What?" Meersa was bewildered. "I do not see—"

Again the Earthman paced the room, teeth clenched, breathing hard.

"You don't forget the past!" he exclaimed suddenly. "You can't. For years my meat and drink have been action—action—action. I've roved two universes. Fought on more planets than I can count. Lived on excitement.

"How do you think I'd fit into being king on a planet like Tela? How do you think I'd enjoy playing guardian to you and your people? I'll tell you, Meersa: I'd go stark, staring mad within a year. I'd hate you all, and I'd abuse you. I'd be a worse dictator than Rsk ever dreamed of being.

"Not because of anything you'd do, either. No. But I couldn't stand the very peace of it all."

"Then what—"

WOLF'S hand swept out in a gesture toward the celestial charts. "I've seen it coming. For the past week the men have been getting the *Ghost* ready to travel again. Right now I'm only waiting for some final figures."

"And what of me?" choked the girl. "Do I go on until my time is come, ruling Tela by myself and hating every lonely minute?"

The raider chief gripped her shoulders.

"Why should you?" he demanded, looking deep into her tear-filled eyes. "You've got a man."

"I? A man? Who?"

"Orcutt."

"Orcutt! That *boy*? When I compare him with you—"

"When you compare him with me, you should thank your lucky stars that you're fortunate enough to have him, my little princess. That boy loves you. He'd cut his own heart out if he thought it would please you. He has a steady head on his shoulders, and brains to fill it. He'll make a king you and your people can be proud of—"

The cabin door opened. Moko, the Uranian scientist, followed by Ivar, entered. The little savant waved a sheaf of papers triumphantly.

"I've got it!" he cried. "I've worked out everything. The whole formula. Route's all planned."

Wolf turned to Ivar.

"What about the supplies?" he demanded. "Is everything on board?"

"The whole works, chief," the big mate nodded. "Crew's on, too."

"Then prepare to blast off!"

"Huh? Now?"

"You heard me! We're leaving. Get a move on!"

Meersa gripped the Earthman's arm. "Wolf! You cannot—"

"On the contrary." He lifted her off her feet, carried her to the forward hatch.

"Good luck, Meersa. Say good-bye to Orcutt for me. And may you and Tela always prosper!"

He set her down on the runway. The hatch swung shut.

She was still standing there, watching the *Ghost* fade into space, when Orcutt ran up.

"They've gone?" he gasped incredulously.

"Yes."

The young Dau stood close behind her, his eyes—like hers—glued on the blurring dot against the sky. His arms slipped about her waist; she did not pull away.

"There goes a man!" he said.

And Meersa nodded.

THE END

If you've enjoyed this book, you will not want to miss these terrific titles…

ARMCHAIR SCI-FI, FANTASY, & HORROR DOUBLE NOVELS, $12.95 each

D-21 **EMPIRE OF EVIL** by Robert Arnette
THE SIGN OF THE TIGER by Alan E. Nourse & J. A. Meyer

D-22 **OPERATION SQUARE PEG** by Frank Belknap Long
ENCHANTRESS OF VENUS by Leigh Brackett

D-23 **THE LIFE WATCH** by Lester Del Rey
CREATURES OF THE ABYSS by Murray Leinster

D-24 **BLACK MAGIC HOLIDAY** by Robert Bloch
STAR HUNTER by Andre Norton

D-25 **EMPIRE OF WOMEN** by John Fletcher
ONE OF OUR CITIES IS MISSING by Irving Cox

D-26 **THE WRONG SIDE OF PARADISE** by Raymond F. Jones
THE INVOLUNTARY IMMORTALS by Rog Phillips

D-27 **EARTH QUARTER** by Damon Knight
ENVOY TO NEW WORLDS by Keith Laumer

D-28 **SLAVES TO THE METAL HORDE** by Milton Lesser
HUNTERS OUT OF TIME by Joseph E. Kelleam

D-29 **RX JUPITER SAVE US** by Ward Moore
BEWARE THE USURPERS by Geoff St. Reynard

D-30 **SECRET OF THE SERPENT** by Don Wilcox
CRUSADE ACROSS THE VOID by Dwight V. Swain

ARMCHAIR SCIENCE FICTION CLASSICS, $12.95 each

C-7 **THE SHAVER MYSTERY, pt. 1**
by Richard S. Shaver

C-8 **THE SHAVER MYSTERY, pt. 2**
by Richard S. Shaver

C-9 **MURDER IN SPACE** by David V. Reed
by David V. Reed

ARMCHAIR MASTERS OF SCIENCE FICTION SERIES, $16.95 each

M-3 **MASTERS OF SCIENCE FICTION, Vol. Three**
Robert Sheckley

M-4 **MASTERS OF SCIENCE FICTION, Vol. Four**
Mack Reynolds, part one

www.ingramcontent.com/pod-product-compliance
Lightning Source LLC
Chambersburg PA
CBHW030310180626
46810CB00003B/1007